VITAMINS AND MINERALS

GENERAL EDITORS

Dale C. Garell, M.D.
Medical Director, California Children Services, Department of Health Services,
County of Los Angeles
Associate Dean for Curriculum; Clinical Professor, Department of Pediatrics &
Family Medicine, University of Southern California School of Medicine
Former President, Society for Adolescent Medicine

Solomon H. Snyder, M.D.
Distinguished Service Professor of Neuroscience, Pharmacology, and Psychiatry, Johns
Hopkins University School of Medicine
Former President, Society for Neuroscience
Albert Lasker Award in Medical Research, 1978

CONSULTING EDITORS

Robert W. Blum, M.D., Ph.D.
Professor and Director, Division of General Pediatrics and Adolescent Health,
University of Minnesota

Charles E. Irwin, Jr., M.D.
Professor of Pediatrics; Director, Division of Adolescent Medicine, University of California, San Francisco

Lloyd J. Kolbe, Ph.D.
Director of the Division of Adolescent and School Health, Center for Chronic
Disease Prevention and Health Promotion, Centers for Disease Control

Jordan J. Popkin
Former Director, Division of Federal Employee Occupational Health, U.S. Public
Health Service Region I

Joseph L. Rauh, M.D.
Professor of Pediatrics and Medicine, Adolescent Medicine, Children's Hospital
Medical Center, Cincinnati
Former President, Society for Adolescent Medicine

THE ENCYCLOPEDIA OF
H E A L T H

THE HEALTHY BODY

Dale C. Garell, M.D. · General Editor

VITAMINS AND MINERALS

Don Nardo

Introduction by C. Everett Koop, M.D., Sc.D.

former Surgeon General, U. S. Public Health Service

CHELSEA HOUSE PUBLISHERS

New York · Philadelphia

The goal of the ENCYCLOPEDIA OF HEALTH *is to provide general information in the ever-changing areas of physiology, psychology, and related medical issues. The titles in this series are not intended to take the place of the professional advice of a physician or other health care professional.*

CHELSEA HOUSE PUBLISHERS
EDITORIAL DIRECTOR   Richard Rennert
EXECUTIVE MANAGING EDITOR   Karyn Gullen Browne
COPY CHIEF   Robin James
PICTURE EDITOR   Adrian G. Allen
ART DIRECTOR   Robert Mitchell
MANUFACTURING DIRECTOR   Gerald Levine
PRODUCTION COORDINATOR   Marie Claire Cebrián-Ume

The Encyclopedia of Health
SENIOR EDITOR   Don Nardo

Staff for VITAMINS AND MINERALS
EDITORIAL ASSISTANT   Mary B. Sisson
PICTURE RESEARCHER   Sandy Jones
DESIGNER   M. Cambraia Magalhães
COVER ILLUSTRATION   Brad Hamann

First Printing
1   3   5   7   9   8   6   4   2

Library of Congress Cataloging-in-Publication Data
Nardo, Don, 1947–
Vitamins and minerals / Don Nardo.
p. cm.—(The Encyclopedia of health. Healthy body)
Includes bibliographical references and index.
ISBN 0-7910-0032-X.
      0-7910-0472-4 (pbk.)
   1. Vitamins—Juvenile literature. Minerals in the body—Juvenile literature. 3. Nutrition—Juvenile literature. [1. Vitamins. 2. Minerals in nutrition. 3. Nutrition.] I. Title.
II. Series.   93-26204
QP771.N36 1994   CIP
613.2—dc20   AC

CONTENTS

THE ENCYCLOPEDIA OF
H E A L T H

THE HEALTHY BODY

The Circulatory System
Dental Health
The Digestive System
The Endocrine System
Exercise
Genetics & Heredity
The Human Body: An Overview
Hygiene
The Immune System
Memory & Learning
The Musculoskeletal System
The Nervous System
Nutrition
The Reproductive System
The Respiratory System
The Senses
Sleep
Speech & Hearing
Sports Medicine
Vision
Vitamins & Minerals

THE LIFE CYCLE

Adolescence
Adulthood
Aging
Childhood
Death & Dying
The Family
Friendship & Love
Pregnancy & Birth

MEDICAL ISSUES

Careers in Health Care
Environmental Health
Folk Medicine
Health Care Delivery
Holistic Medicine
Medical Ethics
Medical Fakes & Frauds
Medical Technology
Medicine & the Law
Occupational Health
Public Health

PSYCHOLOGICAL DISORDERS AND THEIR TREATMENT

Anxiety & Phobias
Child Abuse
Compulsive Behavior
Delinquency & Criminal Behavior
Depression
Diagnosing & Treating Mental Illness
Eating Habits & Disorders
Learning Disabilities
Mental Retardation
Personality Disorders
Schizophrenia
Stress Management
Suicide

MEDICAL DISORDERS AND THEIR TREATMENT

AIDS
Allergies
Alzheimer's Disease
Arthritis
Birth Defects
Cancer
The Common Cold
Diabetes
Emergency Medicine
Gynecological Disorders
Headaches
The Hospital
Kidney Disorders
Medical Diagnosis
The Mind-Body Connection
Mononucleosis and Other Infectious Diseases
Nuclear Medicine
Organ Transplants
Pain
The Physically Challenged
Poisons & Toxins
Prescription & OTC Drugs
Sexually Transmitted Diseases
Skin Disorders
Stroke & Heart Disease
Substance Abuse
Tropical Medicine

PREVENTION AND EDUCATION: THE KEYS TO GOOD HEALTH

C. Everett Koop, M.D., Sc.D.
former Surgeon General,
U.S. Public Health Service

The issue of health education has received particular attention in recent years because of the presence of AIDS in the news. But our response to this particular tragedy points up a number of broader issues that doctors, public health officials, educators, and the public face. In particular, it points up the necessity for sound health education for citizens of all ages.

Over the past 25 years this country has been able to bring about dramatic declines in the death rates for heart disease, stroke, accidents, and for people under the age of 45, cancer. Today, Americans generally eat better and take better care of themselves than ever before. Thus, with the help of modern science and technology, they have a better chance of surviving serious—even catastrophic—illnesses. That's the good news.

But, like every phonograph record, there's a flip side, and one with special significance for young adults. According to a report issued in 1979 by Dr. Julius Richmond, my predecessor as Surgeon General, Americans aged 15 to 24 had a higher death rate in 1979 than they did 20 years earlier. The causes: violent death and injury, alcohol and drug abuse, unwanted pregnancies, and sexually transmitted diseases. Adolescents are particularly vulnerable because they are beginning to explore their own sexuality and perhaps to experiment with drugs. The need for educating young people is critical, and the price of neglect is high.

Yet even for the population as a whole, our health is still far from what it could be. Why? A 1974 Canadian government report attributed all death and disease to four broad elements: inadequacies in the health care system, behavioral factors or unhealthy life-styles, environmental hazards, and human biological factors.

7

To be sure, there are diseases that are still beyond the control of even our advanced medical knowledge and techniques. And despite yearnings that are as old as the human race itself, there is no "fountain of youth" to ward off aging and death. Still, there is a solution to many of the problems that undermine sound health. In a word, that solution is prevention. Prevention, which includes health promotion and education, saves lives, improves the quality of life, and in the long run, saves money.

In the United States, organized public health activities and preventive medicine have a long history. Important milestones in this country or foreign breakthroughs adopted in the United States include the improvement of sanitary procedures and the development of pasteurized milk in the late 19th century and the introduction in the mid-20th century of effective vaccines against polio, measles, German measles, mumps, and other once-rampant diseases. Internationally, organized public health efforts began on a wide-scale basis with the International Sanitary Conference of 1851, to which 12 nations sent representatives. The World Health Organization, founded in 1948, continues these efforts under the aegis of the United Nations, with particular emphasis on combating communicable diseases and the training of health care workers.

Despite these accomplishments, much remains to be done in the field of prevention. For too long, we have had a medical care system that is science- and technology-based, focused, essentially, on illness and mortality. It is now patently obvious that both the social and the economic costs of such a system are becoming insupportable.

Implementing prevention—and its corollaries, health education and pro- motion—is the job of several groups of people.

First, the medical and scientific professions need to continue basic scien- tific research, and here we are making considerable progress. But increased concern with prevention will also have a decided impact on how primary care doctors practice medicine. With a shift to health-based rather than morbidity- based medicine, the role of the "new physician" will include a healthy dose of patient education.

Second, practitioners of the social and behavioral sciences—psycholo- gists, economists, city planners—along with lawyers, business leaders, and government officials—must solve the practical and ethical dilemmas con- fronting us: poverty, crime, civil rights, literacy, education, employment, housing, sanitation, environmental protection, health care delivery systems, and so forth. All of these issues affect public health.

Third is the public at large. We'll consider that very important group in a moment.

Fourth, and the linchpin in this effort, is the public health profession—doctors, epidemiologists, teachers—who must harness the professional expertise of the first two groups and the common sense and cooperation of the third, the public. They must define the problems statistically and qualitatively and then help us set priorities for finding the solutions.

To a very large extent, improving those statistics is the responsibility of every individual. So let's consider more specifically what the role of the individual should be and why health education is so important to that role. First, and most obvious, individuals can protect themselves from illness and injury and thus minimize their need for professional medical care. They can eat nutritious food; get adequate exercise; avoid tobacco, alcohol, and drugs; and take prudent steps to avoid accidents. The proverbial "apple a day keeps the doctor away" is not so far from the truth, after all.

Second, individuals should actively participate in their own medical care. They should schedule regular medical and dental checkups. Should they develop an illness or injury, they should know when to treat themselves and when to seek professional help. To gain the maximum benefit from any medical treatment that they do require, individuals must become partners in that treatment. For instance, they should understand the effects and side effects of medications. I counsel young physicians that there is no such thing as too much information when talking with patients. But the corollary is the patient must know enough about the nuts and bolts of the healing process to understand what the doctor is telling him or her. That is at least partially the patient's responsibility.

Education is equally necessary for us to understand the ethical and public policy issues in health care today. Sometimes individuals will encounter these issues in making decisions about their own treatment or that of family members. Other citizens may encounter them as jurors in medical malpractice cases. But we all become involved, indirectly, when we elect our public officials, from school board members to the president. Should surrogate parenting be legal? To what extent is drug testing desirable, legal, or necessary? Should there be public funding for family planning, hospitals, various types of medical research, and other medical care for the indigent? How should we allocate scant technological resources, such as kidney dialysis and organ transplants? What is the proper role of government in protecting the rights of patients?

What are the broad goals of public health in the United States today? In 1980, the Public Health Service issued a report aptly entitled *Promoting Health—Preventing Disease: Objectives for the Nation*. This report expressed its goals in terms of mortality and in terms of intermediate goals in education and health improvement. It identified 15 major concerns: controlling high blood pressure; improving family planning; improving pregnancy care and infant health; increasing the rate of immunization; controlling sexually transmitted diseases; controlling the presence of toxic agents and radiation in the environment; improving occupational safety and health; preventing accidents; promoting water fluoridation and dental health; controlling infectious diseases; decreasing smoking; decreasing alcohol and drug abuse; improving nutrition; promoting physical fitness and exercise; and controlling stress and violent behavior.

For healthy adolescents and young adults (ages 15 to 24), the specific goal was a 20% reduction in deaths, with a special focus on motor vehicle injuries and alcohol and drug abuse. For adults (ages 25 to 64), the aim was 25% fewer deaths, with a concentration on heart attacks, strokes, and cancers.

Smoking is perhaps the best example of how individual behavior can have a direct impact on health. Today, cigarette smoking is recognized as the single most important preventable cause of death in our society. It is responsible for more cancers and more cancer deaths than any other known agent; is a prime risk factor for heart and blood vessel disease, chronic bronchitis, and emphysema; and is a frequent cause of complications in pregnancies and of babies born prematurely, underweight, or with potentially fatal respiratory and cardiovascular problems.

Since the release of the Surgeon General's first report on smoking in 1964, the proportion of adult smokers has declined substantially, from 43% in 1965 to 30.5% in 1985. Since 1965, 37 million people have quit smoking. Although there is still much work to be done if we are to become a "smoke-free society," it is heartening to note that public health and public education efforts—such as warnings on cigarette packages and bans on broadcast advertising—have already had significant effects.

In 1835, Alexis de Tocqueville, a French visitor to America, wrote, "In America the passion for physical well-being is general." Today, as then, health and fitness are front-page items. But with the greater scientific and technological resources now available to us, we are in a far stronger position to make good health care available to everyone. And with the greater technological threats to us as we approach the 21st century, the need to do so is more urgent than ever before. Comprehensive information about basic biology, preventive medicine, medical and surgical treatments, and related ethical and public policy issues can help you arm yourself with the knowledge you need to be healthy throughout your life.

FOREWORD

Dale C. Garell, M.D.

Advances in our understanding of health and disease during the 20th century have been truly remarkable. Indeed, it could be argued that modern health care is one of the greatest accomplishments in all of human history. In the early 20th century, improvements in sanitation, water treatment, and sewage disposal reduced death rates and increased longevity. Previously untreatable illnesses can now be managed with antibiotics, immunizations, and modern surgical techniques. Discoveries in the fields of immunology, genetic diagnosis, and organ transplantation are revolutionizing the prevention and treatment of disease. Modern medicine is even making inroads against cancer and heart disease, two of the leading causes of death in the United States.

Although there is much to be proud of, medicine continues to face enormous challenges. Science has vanquished diseases such as smallpox and polio, but new killers, most notably AIDS, confront us. Moreover, we now victimize ourselves with what some have called "diseases of choice," or those brought on by drug and alcohol abuse, bad eating habits, and mismanagement of the stresses and strains of contemporary life. The very technology that is doing so much to prolong life has brought with it previously unimaginable ethical dilemmas related to issues of death and dying. The rising cost of health care is a matter of central concern to us all. And violence in the form of automobile accidents, homicide, and suicide remains the major killer of young adults.

In the past, most people were content to leave health care and medical treatment in the hands of professionals. But since the 1960s, the consumer of medical care—that is, the patient—has assumed an increasingly central role in the management of his or her own health. There has also been a new emphasis placed on prevention: People are recognizing that their own actions can help prevent many of the conditions that have caused death and disease in the past. This accounts for the growing commitment to good nutrition and regular exercise, for the increasing number of people who are choosing not to smoke, and for a new moderation in people's drinking habits.

People want to know more about themselves and their own health. They are curious about their body: its anatomy, physiology, and biochemistry. They want to keep up with rapidly evolving medical technologies and procedures. They are willing to educate themselves about common disorders and diseases so that they can be full partners in their own health care.

THE ENCYCLOPEDIA OF HEALTH is designed to provide the basic knowledge that readers will need if they are to take significant responsibility for their own health. It is also meant to serve as a frame of reference for further study and exploration. The encyclopedia is divided into five subsections: The Healthy Body; The Life Cycle; Medical Disorders & Their Treatment; Psychological Disorders & Their Treatment; and Medical Issues. For each topic covered by the encyclopedia, we present the essential facts about the relevant biology; the symptoms, diagnosis, and treatment of common diseases and disorders; and ways in which you can prevent or reduce the severity of health problems when that is possible. The encyclopedia also projects what may lie ahead in the way of future treatment or prevention strategies.

The broad range of topics and issues covered in the encyclopedia reflects that human health encompasses physical, psychological, social, environmental, and spiritual well-being. Just as the mind and the body are inextricably linked, so, too, is the individual an integral part of the wider world that comprises his or her family, society, and environment. To discuss health in its broadest aspect it is necessary to explore the many ways in which it is connected to such fields as law, social science, public policy, economics, and even religion. And so, the encyclopedia is meant to be a bridge between science, medical technology, the world at large, and you. I hope that it will inspire you to pursue in greater depth particular areas of interest and that you will take advantage of the suggestions for further reading and the lists of resources and organizations that can provide additional information.

CHAPTER 1

THE DISCOVERY OF VITAMINS AND MINERALS

A young girl at the Salem witch trials faints after making an accusation of witchcraft. Some commentators have speculated that such hysteria was in part caused by vitamin deficiencies.

In 1497, the Portuguese explorer Vasco da Gama set sail on an epic voyage of discovery. By the following year, he had managed to find a route around Africa to India, opening opportunities for trade between Europe and southern Asia. Despite this triumph, da Gama's expedition met with tragedy on the way back. Because of unfavorable winds, the explorer and his crew wandered around the Arabian Sea, west of India, for three months. After the first several weeks, many crewmen became ill. First, they lost their appetite, grew weak, and began to complain of aches in their muscles and joints. As the weeks rolled on, some of the men developed small hemorrhages, or bleeding sores, on their skin, especially around their eyes, and then their gums began swelling and bleeding. Eventually, most of the sick men could no longer perform even the smallest physical tasks. They just lay around in a miserable, painful stupor until most of them died. At the end of the three months, nearly the entire crew was suffering various symptoms of the illness and it seemed as though the expedition would end in failure. But then the men reached land and, after a week or two, all of the survivors completely recovered.

The sailors were familiar with the sickness that had struck them. They called it the *scurvy*, a disease that, since ancient times, had afflicted seamen on long voyages in which they stayed away from land for long periods of time. And just as they were not the first to come down with scurvy, da Gama's men were not the last. For example, when French navigator Jacques Cartier sailed across the Atlantic Ocean and explored Newfoundland in 1535, many of his men contracted the disease and died. Scurvy continued to take its toll on many naval and exploratory voyages in the centuries that followed. All of those who suffered from the disease had one thing in common. They had no idea what caused it or how to cure it.

Eliminating Scurvy

The first systematic treatment for scurvy began in the 1700s. In 1758, a hard-working Scottish doctor named James Lind took charge of the British Royal Navy's Haslar Naval Hospital in Hampshire, England. At the time, scurvy was so common among British sailors that more men died of the disease than perished in wartime. Appalled by this high mortality rate, Lind became determined to find a cure for scurvy.

After trying a number of different remedies, none of which worked, Lind read that large numbers of Dutch sailors did not suffer from the illness. What caused so many Dutch sailors to be immune, while seamen of other nationalities suffered in great numbers, Lind wondered? Among a number of factors, he considered the sailors' diet. Since the 1560s, he found, many Dutch ships had been taking along fresh fruit on long voyages, something vessels from other lands did not do. As an experiment, in 1795 Lind persuaded the British to prescribe regular doses of lemon juice for all seamen. In the space of only a few weeks, the dreaded scurvy disappeared from the British navy. For this achievement and for other important medical advances that improved the health of sailors, Lind eventually came to be called the founder of English naval hygiene.

Although Lind had discovered that some element in fruit juices, especially citrus juices, prevented scurvy, he did not know what that element was. At the time, scientists knew very little about the chemical makeup of the various foods people ate. Today, scientists know that the preventative element in juices that eluded Lind is called ascorbic acid, more commonly known as vitamin C, one of a number of nutrient substances called *vitamins* and *minerals.* These are chemical compounds the body requires in small amounts to maintain regular health and promote growth and reproduction.

The Poor Commonly Afflicted

For thousands of years before the 20th century, without realizing it, people regularly observed the physical effects of vitamins and minerals in their diets. Either they took in the required amounts of these substances and enjoyed good health, or, as in the case of sailors and scurvy, they took in too little and experienced serious illness. Often, they searched for and found cures for these ailments without knowing why these cures worked.

The ancient Egyptians, for example, recognized a condition called *night blindness,* the inability of the eyes to adjust to dim illumination. A well-known surviving Egyptian document, the Ebers Papyrus, records a night blindness cure in which juice from an animal's liver was squirted directly into the eyes. Later, the Greek physician Hippocrates, often called the father of medicine, cured night blindness by prescribing the eating of raw ox liver. Scientists now know why these treatments were sometimes successful. Night blindness is a common symptom of vitamin A deficiency and raw liver contains considerable amounts of that nutrient.

Vitamin A deficiencies in ancient times occurred mainly among the poor, who often could not afford to eat meat or green leafy vegetables,

The Ebers Papyrus, which records a cure for night blindness involving the application of the secretions of an animal liver directly into the eyes.

both of which contain plentiful amounts of the vitamin. A similar situation developed in the early 1700s when the Spanish introduced corn cultivation to Europe. Soon, because it was easy and inexpensive to grow, the poorer classes in Spain and some other countries began to subsist almost entirely on corn. Before long, many peasants began to notice rough, red, and itchy patches on the skin. They also suffered from abdominal pains and diarrhea. Because of the redness of the skin, some Spanish physicians coined the name *mal de la rosa,* or "sickness of the rose," for the new illness. The Italians called it *pellagra,* or "rough skin," the term still used today to describe the condition, which is now known to result from a deficiency of a vitamin called niacin.

The Seaweed Cure

The health effects of minerals were also observed and experimented with for many centuries. The ancient Chinese, for instance, found a successful treatment for *goiter,* a condition brought on by a lack of the mineral iodine in the diet. Iodine is essential for normal functioning of the thyroid gland, located in the throat, and a lack of iodine causes the gland to swell, sometimes into a lump many inches in diameter. Children suffering from this condition can become mentally retarded. Over the course of time, the Chinese developed a folk remedy for goiter—eating seaweed. The Chinese had no idea at the time, of course, that the remedy worked because seaweed has high concentrations of iodine.

The first person to recognize that iodine helps cure goiter was the English chemist William Prout. In 1816, he successfully used doses of the mineral to treat several patients suffering from the illness. This was one of the first instances of scientific recognition that small amounts of certain dietary substances might be essential for normal health.

More solid evidence for this idea came in the late 1800s when doctors and scientists from several countries tried to find treatments for *beriberi.* This disease is characterized by fatigue, difficulty in walking, and swelling and even paralysis of the nerves. In 1882, a Japanese doctor named Kanechiro Takaki successfully treated sailors suffering from beriberi by adding meat and vegetables to their diet, which before had consisted mainly of rice. Takaki concluded that some substance that keeps people from contracting the disease is present in meat and vegetables but not in rice.

On the Trail of the Beriberi Cure

Takaki's conclusion turned out to be only partly right. He did not realize that beriberi is caused by a lack of the vitamin thiamine, which does exist in rice. But the thiamine collects in the outer shell, or hull, of the rice, and many people in Asia, including the Japanese, regularly removed and discarded the hulls, a process known as polishing. People whose diets consisted mainly of *polished rice* were much more likely to contract beriberi than those who consumed their rice whole.

The Dutch scientist Christiaan Eijkman suspected this was the case. In 1897, while working in the Dutch East Indies, a region now called Indonesia, he studied and described a disease of chickens that is very similar to beriberi. To test his theory about rice hulls, he fed polished rice exclusively to one group of chickens and unpolished rice to a second group. Eijkman found that the first group quickly developed beriberi but that the second group remained healthy. What is more, when he fed the discarded hulls to the sick chickens, most of them got well. This proved that some kind of beriberi-fighting substance was in the rice hulls.

In 1912, Casimir Funk, a Polish biochemist, tried to take Eijkman's work a step further and isolate the mysterious substance in the rice hulls. Funk performed many experiments, all of them unsuccessful. However, he remained convinced that the substance existed. He believed it was one of a group of chemical compounds called amines. Deficiencies of certain special amines, he theorized, caused not only beriberi, but also illnesses like scurvy and pellagra. At first, he called these special substances vital amines, but after using the term for some time, he ran the words together, forming the contraction *vitamine*. In 1914, Funk published his ideas about these substances in a book titled *The Vitamines*.

A British biochemist named Frederick G. Hopkins was working on the same idea about special food nutrients at about the same time as

The British biochemist Frederick G. Hopkins, who along with the Polish biochemist Casimir Funk is credited with the discovery that certain illnesses are caused by deficiencies of chemical substances in the body.

Funk. To distinguish them from well-recognized "basic food factors" like carbohydrates, fats, and proteins, Hopkins called the unknown nutrients accessory food factors. Although he and Funk called them by different names, they were describing the same substances. In the following few years, scientists adopted Funk's word, dropping the final *e* and calling the substances vitamins. Funk and Hopkins shared credit for formulating the theory that lack of certain vitamins, and also certain minerals, causes deficiency diseases such as beriberi.

The Research Continues

After Funk and Hopkins, the most important pioneer in the discovery of the role of vitamins and minerals in diet was the American biochemist and educator Elmer V. McCollum. At first, most scientists thought that only two vitamins existed, one soluble, or able to be dissolved, in water, the other soluble in fat. In 1913, working at the University of Wisconsin, McCollum discovered vitamin A, a *fat-soluble* substance. Two years later, he suggested that there are really many other vitamins of each type and he proved this in experiments over the next seven years. He not only showed that these substances exist, but also explained some of their physical functions. For example, he was the first person to describe vitamin D and establish the role it plays in bone formation.

McCollum published some of his new findings in 1918 in a book titled *The Newer Knowledge of Nutrition,* now considered a classic study of vitamins. In addition to his isolation, description, and study of various vitamins, McCollum devised the now-familiar system of identifying these chemicals with letters. Today, although most are still identified in this manner, some, like niacin and thiamine, are not. McCollum also studied and explained the complex roles of the minerals calcium and magnesium in human diet.

Other scientists carried on McCollum's work and continued to study vitamins and minerals. By 1948, with the discovery of vitamin B_{12}, all of the vitamins presently recognized by scientists had been discovered. And scientists had learned a great deal about how minerals

The American biochemist Elmer V. McCollum, who is credited with the discovery of vitamins A and D.

such as iodine, phosphorus, and zinc help to maintain many important body processes.

However, despite these advances, and others that occurred in the years that followed, scientists do not yet fully understand how and why certain vitamins and minerals work. Research continues in labs around the world, some of it directed toward finding out more about the known vitamins, and some toward possibly identifying new varieties. Scientists are also studying how unusually large doses of vitamins affect the body. For example, some research in recent years has suggested that *megadoses* of vitamin C might help reduce a person's susceptibility to catching colds. There is still considerable disagreement about this and other vitamin-related issues. All of the researchers in the field agree on one point, however. They realize that the human body is a highly complex organism in which hundreds of different substances function in varying amounts and ways to ensure proper growth and health, and that a complete understanding of nutrition is still many years away.

CHAPTER 2

VITAMINS: THE BODY'S ESSENTIAL ABCs

The labels on food containers provide consumers with much valuable information about the nutritional content of what they eat.

Vitamins are essential to the human body. They help regulate the chemical reactions the body utilizes to convert food into energy and living tissue. In general, vitamins affect the body's chemical reactions without themselves being altered by these reactions. Therefore, scientists often refer to vitamins as *catalysts,* which are substances that retain their own physical characteristics while changing the speed and nature of chemical reactions.

One vital chemical process that vitamins help regulate is the conversion of carbohydrates, fats, and proteins into energy. In this case, some vitamins act as *enzymes,* or substances that alter the structure of the molecules in the foodstuffs. While these chemical changes are occurring, energy is released, energy the body uses to work the muscles, digest food, and maintain normal brain functions. Vitamins also aid in cell division, body growth, and maintaining eyesight. In addition, they contribute to the wound-healing process by helping blood to clot properly. Without vitamins, most of these important bodily processes would occur very slowly or cease completely. Not surprisingly, then, prolonged lack of essential vitamins leads to serious deficiency diseases, such as scurvy and beriberi, and eventually to death.

Amounts and Kinds of Vitamins

Unlike some other essential food substances, such as proteins and carbohydrates, of which the body needs large regular supplies, vitamins are needed in relatively tiny quantities. Vitamin doses are usually measured by the *milligram,* or one-thousandth of a *gram.* While the body stores some vitamins in moderate quantities, others must be taken in on a regular basis. This can be accomplished by eating a well-balanced diet containing items from varied food groups such as fruits and vegetables, grains and starches, dairy products, and meats and fish. Many people also take vitamin supplements, usually in pill form.

The amounts of various vitamins that the body needs daily, referred to as the recommended dietary allowances, or RDAs, have been established by the National Research Council's Food and Nutrition Board. In most cases, adults, because their bodies are larger, need more daily doses of vitamins than children do. For example, the RDA of vitamin C for adults is 60 milligrams, while that for children ages one to fourteen is 45–50 milligrams. Also, men, because their body masses are usually greater than women's, generally have higher RDAs of vitamins than women do.

Scientists usually group the vitamins into two general categories— those soluble in fat and those soluble in water. The fat-soluble vitamins, A, D, E, and K, are absorbed into the body in various kinds of dietary fats, including those in meats and dairy products. The body stores these vitamins in its fatty tissue and, therefore, they are not regularly excreted in the urine. Since the body usually maintains a small store of the fat-soluble vitamins, it is not often necessary to replenish them on a daily basis.

The *water-soluble* vitamins, on the other hand, are not stored in the body. These substances, including vitamin C and the B-complex vitamins, do get excreted in small quantities in the urine and, therefore, the body must have fairly regular fresh supplies of them. Water-soluble vitamins are also less stable in the presence of heat than the fat-soluble variety. That means that water-soluble vitamins are more likely to be lost during the cooking and processing of foods. Thus, people who consume large quantities of highly cooked or processed foods, as opposed, for example, to fresh, uncooked fruits and vegetables, may not be getting enough vitamin C or other water-soluble vitamins.

Vitamin A—Essential for Growth

A closer examination of a few selected vitamins, including their functions and sources, demonstrates their vital importance to the body. Vitamin A—also called retinol—is one of the body's most essential substances. This vitamin aids in the growth and development of bones and teeth, especially in unborn babies and young children. Therefore, without vitamin A, people and other animals could not grow in a normal, healthy manner. The vitamin also helps maintain the *epithelial tissues,* the topmost skin layers both inside and outside the body. As health expert Martha Davis Dunn comments in her book *Fundamentals of Nutrition,* vitamin A:

> is essential for normal external epithelial tissues. This involves the outer layer of the skin and the layer lining the mucous membranes [soft, moist areas such as the inside of the nose]. Other epithelial tissues are found

in the mouth, the eyes, the respiratory tract, and genito-
urinary tract. Vitamin A promotes the growth of epithelial cells for the development and maintenance of
tissue.

Vitamin A not only promotes the growth of such epithelial tissues, but
also helps keep these tissues free from infection. For example, a lack
of the vitamin can cause a skin condition known as xerophthalmia, in
which the surface of the eye becomes very dry and open to local

infection. In addition, vitamin A is involved in the formation of certain pigments that allow the eyes to function correctly when light varies in intensity. Therefore, a deficiency of the vitamin can lead to night blindness, the inability to see normally in reduced light.

Vitamin A occurs only in animals. Therefore, common sources of the substance are egg yolk, liver, milk, and butter. However, certain plants contain substances known as provitamin A carotenoids, or *carotenes,* which are, in a sense, incomplete forms of the vitamin. The bodies of people and animals who ingest carotenes transform the

Milk, cheese, and dairy products are rich in vitamin A.

substances into complete and usable vitamin A. Among the fruits and vegetables that contain carotenes are dark green, leafy vegetables like spinach; deep yellow vegetables such as carrots, sweet potatoes, and winter squash; and deep yellow fruits, including cantaloupe and dried apricots. Once vitamin A enters or forms in the body, it becomes stored in the liver, which contains more than 90% of the body's supply of the substance.

Vitamin E—Oxygen Fighter

Vitamin E, also known as tocopherol, is another important fat-soluble vitamin. It is found in many foods, the best sources being whole grains, lettuce, vegetable oils, liver, beans, meat, and fish. For many years, scientists were unsure of exactly what vitamin E does for the body. The first discovery was that the substance helps protect vitamins A and C, as well as natural acids occurring in fat, from *oxidation.* Oxidation is a chemical process in which oxygen molecules corrode and eventually destroy other substances. For example, common rust forms from the oxidation of metals when exposed to oxygen in the air. Similarly, various substances in the body can be oxidized by certain kinds of oxygen molecules that move through the blood system. Vitamin E acts as an antioxidant, or a substance that counteracts oxidation. In addition to protecting other vitamins from being destroyed, vitamin E also prevents body fats from turning rancid due to oxidation. And because the membranes surrounding the body's billions of cells contain a high percentage of fatty acids that could readily become oxidized, the vitamin helps protect these membranes from weakening.

In the late 1980s and early 1990s, vitamin E became increasingly controversial as scientific studies began to show that it might have even more beneficial antioxidizing powers. According to studies reported in May 1993 in the *New England Journal of Medicine,* the vitamin, if taken in supplements on a regular basis, may help prevent heart attacks and diseases of the heart and arteries. In one of the studies, which involved some 120,000 people, those who took regular vitamin E supplements had 40% fewer cases of heart disease than those who did not.

Researchers say that this positive result can be explained by the discovery in recent years that oxidation plays a bigger role in causing heart disease than doctors once realized. For decades, the chief culprit has been LDL, a "bad" form of *cholesterol,* a white fatty substance found in meats and dairy products. The LDL can collect inside arterial walls, narrowing the vessels and leading to blood-flow problems and sometimes heart attacks. These recent studies have shed new light on this process. Medical writer Geoffrey Cowley reported in *Newsweek* magazine:

> Researchers have known for some time that high cho-
> lesterol isn't the whole story on heart disease. Dr.
> Daniel Steinberg, a cardiologist at the University of
> California, San Diego, theorized more than a decade
> ago that oxidation . . . can . . . damage coronary arteries.
> . . . The process has been implicated in everything from
> cataracts to cancer—and researchers suspect it is what
> makes LDL, the bad form of cholesterol, so dangerous.
> Steinberg and others have shown that when LDL lodges
> in arterial walls and becomes oxidized, it not only
> damages nearby tissues but attracts white blood cells.
> The white cells gorge themselves on oxidized LDL and
> accumulate within the arterial lining, causing plaques
> [thick deposits] that narrow the arteries. The resulting
> loss of blood flow can cause everything from chest
> pain to heart attacks.

The new studies seem to show that vitamin E renders the loose oxygen molecules harmless, thus sharply reducing oxidation, and, in turn, the buildup of plaque in the arteries. Patients in the studies took vitamin E supplements containing doses of at least 100 IUs (vitamin E is measured in international units) per day. This is about eight times the current RDA for the vitamin. Some doctors feel that the studies are still preliminary and that further research must be done before vitamin E's benefits for heart disease are conclusive. But there is widespread optimism in the medical community. "All studies point in the same direction," says Dr. John LaRosa, a medical researcher at George Washington University. "It's very exciting because things like vitamin E are not all that expensive compared to the drugs that are used to treat

Whole grains are a rich source of vitamin E.

cholesterol." Indeed, a two-month supply of 100- or 200-unit doses of the vitamin costs less than six dollars at many pharmacies. This low cost, along with increased public awareness about vitamin E's benefits, caused a rise in U.S. sales of the substance from $260 million in 1990 to $392 million in 1992.

Vitamin C—Maintaining the Body's Structural Integrity

Like the fat-soluble vitamins, the water-soluble vitamins are essential to the body. Perhaps the best known and most widely discussed of the water-soluble vitamins is vitamin C, also called ascorbic acid. The best dietary sources of this substance are citrus fruits such as oranges and lemons, as well as tomatoes, cantaloupe, potatoes, strawberries, and raw cabbage. The key word here, as in the case of cabbage, is raw, because the vitamin is rendered ineffective by heat. Exposure to oxygen, iron, and copper also reduces the potency of vitamin C. The best way to store vitamin C–rich fruits and vegetables is in a refrigerator bin that keeps them cold and in minimal contact with air.

In addition to preventing the deficiency disease scurvy, vitamin C aids in the formation of a tough, fibrous tissue called collagen. Since collagen is a major component of bones, teeth, cartilage, connective tissues, skin, and the walls of tiny blood vessels, the vitamin is absolutely essential to the structural integrity of the body. Tooth and bone formation, as well as the healing of skin wounds, burns, and bone fractures—all processes that utilize collagen—could not occur without vitamin C.

The vitamin also helps metabolize, or break down, *amino acids* in foods consumed by the body. Amino acids are the building blocks of proteins. Thus, vitamin C aids in the conversion of raw protein into a form the body can readily use to make new muscle tissue. In addition, the vitamin enhances the absorption of iron from the digestive tract into the bloodstream. It is not surprising, then, that individuals who lack the proper amount of vitamin C often suffer from a deficiency of iron.

Though most people associate vitamin C with citrus fruits, other fruits, such as tomatoes, and vegetables are rich in this vitamin.

The daily dosage of vitamin C necessary for good health is still being debated among researchers. As Maurice E. Shils and Vernon R. Young note in their book *Modern Nutrition in Health and Disease:*

> The supply of vitamin C necessary to offer protection against scurvy is about 10 milligrams daily. However . . . [the amount] required to attain optimum health is a matter of controversy. . . . Therefore, it is not surprising that different recommended dietary allowances (RDAs) exist for the various countries, ranging between 30 milligrams and 120 milligrams.

The RDA of vitamin C in the United States falls about midway in this range—60 milligrams for adults and 45–50 milligrams for children.

This level of the vitamin is safe and easily attainable. A single orange contains about 66 milligrams of vitamin C, a cup of orange juice 100 milligrams, half of a cantaloupe 90 milligrams, and a baked potato 31 milligrams.

The B-Complex Vitamins—Metabolizing Foods

Scientists originally thought that the water-soluble vitamin B complex was one vitamin. Later, they discovered that the complex actually consists of eight separate vitamins. These are thiamine, or vitamin B_1; riboflavin, or vitamin B_2; niacin; vitamin B_6; pantothenic acid; biotin; vitamin B_{12}; and folic acid.

In general, the B-complex vitamins are important in metabolizing foods. Thiamine, found in green vegetables, meat, nuts, soybeans, yeasts, and grains, and niacin, found in fish, green vegetables, poultry, and grains, are both required by the body to break down carbohydrates for use as energy. Thus, thiamine and niacin are essential because they release the energy the body needs for growth, movement, and the maintenance and repair of tissues. Pantothenic acid, the best sources of which are liver, egg yolk, broccoli, meat, nuts, and grains, also aids in converting carbohydrates into energy and helps break down fats and amino acids.

Riboflavin, like thiamine and niacin, helps metabolize carbohydrates, and, like pantothenic acid, aids in the breakdown of fats. Unlike the others, riboflavin also works to metabolize proteins. And riboflavin is essential for normal cell function because it allows the cells to utilize energy for their routine chemical processes. This nutrient, which is abundant in eggs, fish, milk, poultry, and green vegetables, is extremely important in maintaining healthy skin, eyes, and the nervous system.

Both vitamin B_6 and biotin help break down amino acids, as well as carbohydrates and fats. In addition, vitamin B_6 aids in the process the body employs to synthesize, or create, certain nonessential but useful amino acids. Because of its key involvement in these and other chemical processes that affect the body's nerve tissues, vitamin B_6 is an essential component of a healthy nervous system. It is available in

yeast, grains, fish, and most vegetables, while biotin is found in egg yolk, nuts, liver, and most vegetables. Bacteria normally found in the human intestines also produce small amounts of biotin.

Vitamin B_{12} and folic acid are essential to normal reproduction because they are required in the production of *DNA,* the chemical substance within cells that carries the genetic "blueprints" of life.

Green vegetables contain thiamine and niacin, two of the B-complex vitamins.

Without these vitamins, therefore, animal species could not reproduce and life would be impossible. Vitamin B_{12} occurs in only tiny amounts in plants, so the best sources of the vitamin are animal products such as meat, seafood, liver, kidney, eggs, and milk. Folic acid is found in green leafy vegetables, beans, nuts, yeast, meat, and fish. While vitamin B_{12} survives the cooking process fairly well, folic acid does not.

Spelling Life and Health

It is clear from these brief descriptions of some of the vitamins that these substances, though utilized by the body in extremely tiny quantities, are absolutely vital in maintaining regular bodily functions, as well as good health. Without vitamin B_{12}, vitamin A, and thiamine, reproduction and growth could not occur, and without vitamins C and E, the body's cell and tissue structure could not be maintained. Other vitamins are equally important. For example, vitamin D, often called the sunshine vitamin because it forms in the skin when the body is exposed to sunlight, helps the body metabolize calcium and phosphorus for healthy bones and teeth. And vitamin K is essential for blood clotting. Exemplifying the old adage that "good things come in small packages," vitamins are the microscopic ABCs that spell life and health for people and animals.

CHAPTER 3

LACKING THE ESSENTIALS: VITAMIN DEFICIENCIES

A 19th-century drawing of a young man suffering from cretinism. Some forms of mental retardation are thought to be the result of vitamin deficiencies.

A vitamin deficiency is a lack of the minimum amount of a certain vitamin needed by the body to maintain regular good health. If prolonged vitamin deficiency occurs, a deficiency disease can develop. As described earlier, such diseases, including scurvy and beriberi, have been known since the beginning of recorded history and came to be understood by scientists only in the last two centuries. Thus, systematic studies of and treatments for these diseases are a relatively recent development.

Some vitamin deficiency diseases used to be quite common in certain geographic areas. For example, beriberi, caused by a lack of the vitamin thiamine, was prevalent in southeastern Asia and what is now Indonesia, areas where people regularly polished their rice and, in the process, unknowingly discarded the vitamin along with the rice hulls. Today, thanks to increased knowledge about nutrition and government programs that bring that knowledge to large populations, the occurrence of beriberi has become rare in Asia.

Similarly, the majority of vitamin deficiency diseases have become quite rare in most other parts of the world. This is especially true in the developed, or industrialized, countries such as the United States, Canada, Australia, and most European nations. In these countries, advanced medical knowledge and education about nutrition, combined with access to well-rounded, nutritious diets, has greatly reduced the number of reported cases of such diseases. In the United States, for example, most of the rare cases of scurvy, the disease caused by lack of vitamin C, occur in babies and elderly people, groups that occasionally experience periods of inadequate diet.

In some other parts of the world, on the other hand, usually in poorer, un- or semi-developed nations, vitamin deficiencies are, unfortunately, still common. These are almost invariably areas in which poverty, drought, and the ravages of prolonged war and social instability have combined to bring on widespread famine. The best known and most tragic examples are in African countries like the Sudan, Somalia, and Ethiopia. Large numbers of people in these nations continue to suffer from deficiencies of many vitamins, contributing to a general condition of malnutrition, or lack of proper diet and nutrition. Despite large-scale attempts in the 1980s and early 1990s by the United Nations and several humanitarian groups to help alleviate these problems, millions of people remain affected and thousands die each month.

Counteracting Vitamin C Deficiency

Scurvy is one of the most prevalent vitamin deficiency illnesses found in famine-ravaged areas. Some of the early symptoms, or physical signs, of the disease are a decrease in the amount and frequency of urination, a general feeling of weakness, and poor appetite. If a lack of vitamin C in the diet continues, other symptoms may follow. One of these is iron anemia, or the lack of the proper amount of iron in the blood, directly resulting from the lack of vitamin C which helps the body metabolize iron. Other symptoms are swollen and inflamed gums, loosened teeth, swollen wrist and ankle joints, shortness of breath, and increased tendencies to develop bone fractures and infections. All of these symptoms are linked, in one way or another, to the weakening and destruction of collagen, the body's important structural material, which cannot form and remain healthy without vitamin C.

In general, increasing one's intake of vitamin C will reverse the effects of scurvy. As mentioned earlier, the illness does occasionally occur in developed countries, usually in infants, when it is often referred to as Barlow's disease. Most often, mild cases of the illness appear soon after a baby ceases breast feeding if the foods that replace the mother's milk lack sufficient amounts of vitamin C. The best way to counteract the condition is to feed the child orange or tomato juice once or twice a day. Likewise, elderly people whose diets have become deficient in vitamin C need only drink these juices or to eat an orange, tomato, cantaloupe, or some other fruit containing the vitamin each day. More severe cases of scurvy, those resulting from prolonged intake of less than 10 milligrams of vitamin C a day, may require treatment with higher doses of the vitamin, in the form of tablets that can be either chewed or swallowed. In the worst cases, doctors attempt to treat other symptoms of vitamin C deficiency, such as broken bones, bleeding gums, or infections, separately and simultaneously.

An interesting footnote to the occurrence of vitamin C deficiency is the fact that people who smoke cigarettes are more likely than nonsmokers to become deficient in the vitamin. This is because smoking reduces the body's ability to absorb, use, and store vitamin C.

Apparently, chemicals in cigarette smoke, including nicotine, tend to oxidize much of the vitamin C in the smoker's body. According to doctors, average smokers may need twice as much vitamin C in their diets as nonsmokers, or at least 120 milligrams of the vitamin daily. For this reason, it seems prudent for smokers to take vitamin C supplements regularly while they make a concerted effort to quit the habit, which, it has been widely proven, also causes many other health problems.

Lack of Thiamine and Niacin

Beriberi is one of the most destructive vitamin deficiency diseases, especially in cases of prolonged lack of thiamine in the diet. Initial symptoms include fatigue, depression, emotional instability, and loss of appetite. A person also may display irritability, a loss of interest in normal, daily tasks, and, in the case of children, a retardation of normal growth. As thiamine deficiency continues, the physical effects become more severe. For one thing, the sheaths of tissue surrounding the nerves begin to degenerate, causing pain and eventually paralysis of the muscles. Prolonged lack of thiamine also weakens the heart, a condition sometimes referred to as wet beriberi. Other symptoms of full-blown beriberi are severe constipation, indigestion, and *anorexia,* a condition in which a person becomes thin and undernourished as a result of reduced food intake.

Although the most severe cases of thiamine deficiency generally occur in impoverished countries where famine is common, doctors in the United States and other developed countries regularly see some milder, but still serious, cases. Usually, these patients are alcoholics who suffer from the deficiency because they tend to substitute alcohol for nutritious foods in their diets. The best treatment is to reduce the amount of alcohol consumed and increase intake of thiamine-rich foods such as poultry, pork, eggs, fish, beans, peas, and peanuts. The RDA of thiamine in the United States is about 1 milligram per day, approximately the amount present in two cups of black-eyed peas or eight ounces of baked ham. This dosage of the vitamin easily eliminates the risk of deficiency.

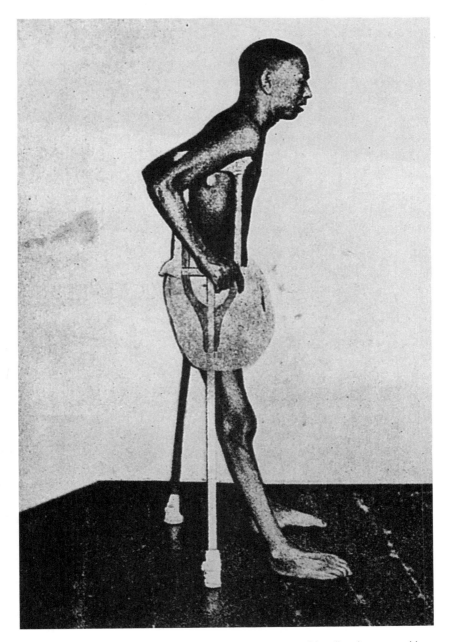

This Indonesian man suffers from a severe case of beriberi, caused by a lack of thiamine, or vitamin B1.

Pellagra, the disease that became common in the 1700s among poor Europeans who subsisted mainly on corn, results from a prolonged deficiency of another B-complex vitamin—niacin. Although rare in developed countries, cases of niacin deficiency are still fairly common in sections of poor countries in which people's diets lack meats, fish, dairy products, yeast, and green vegetables. According to nutritionists Marie V. Krause and L. Kathleen Mahan:

The effects of pellagra, caused by a deficiency of niacin.

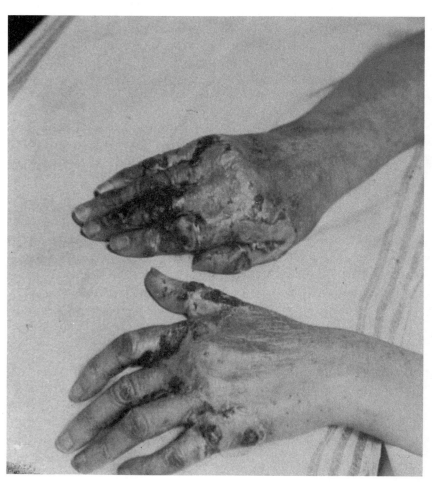

The symptoms of niacin deficiency are many. In the early stages muscular weakness, anorexia, indigestion and skin eruptions occur. Severe deficiency of niacin leads to pellagra which is characterized by dermatitis [a skin condition], dementia [emotional and mental disorder], diarrhea (the "3 D's" of pellagra), tremors [shaking], and sore tongue. . . . The skin develops a cracked pigmented scaly dermatitis. . . . Lesions [sores] appear in many parts of the central nervous system resulting in confusion, disorientation. . . . Many digestive abnormalities develop in niacin deficiency causing irritation and inflammation of the mucous membranes of the mouth and the gastrointestinal [digestive] tract. Clinical symptoms of severe riboflavin deficiency appear. In fact many of the niacin deficiencies are similar, owing to the close interrelationships of riboflavin and niacin in cell metabolism.

Once pellagra develops, doctors must combine vitamin therapy, that is, large doses of niacin, with more specific treatments for damaged skin and various kinds of sores. Of course, it is preferable to avoid getting the disease in the first place and it is easily avoided. Because niacin is found in varying amounts in many foods, the best way to avoid niacin deficiency is to eat a well-balanced diet that includes items from several different food groups. As might be expected, this maxim applies to other vitamins as well.

The Vital Link Between Vitamin D and Calcium

A deficiency of vitamin D can also be serious. This is because the vitamin is vital in metabolizing the mineral calcium, a major component of the bones and teeth. A lack of vitamin D results in the body absorbing from foods less calcium than it needs, and this calcium shortfall weakens the bones. This effect is most serious in children because their bones are still growing and forming. A severe deficiency of vitamin D can lead to a disease called *rickets*. Typical symptoms include fragile bones, malformed skeleton, bowlegs, knock-knees, rib deformities, and enlarged knees, elbows, and other joints.

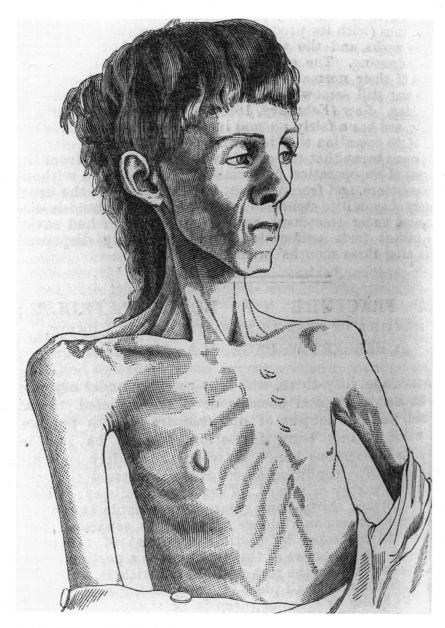

A late 19th-century illustration of a woman suffering from anorexia nervosa, a condition aggravated by lack of niacin in the diet.

Rickets was a fairly common health problem in the United States until the early 1920s, when scientists isolated vitamin D and realized its importance to the body. Although fewer cases of the disease are reported today in this country, minor deficiencies of the vitamin are still commonplace. This is because vitamin D occurs less frequently in foods than any other vitamin. The two main sources of the substance are sunshine, which is absorbed through the skin and converted into vitamin D, and fish-liver oils. Almost all other foods that contain the vitamin have tiny and nearly useless traces of it. Since the amount of exposure to sunlight and consumption of fish vary widely among cultures, populations, age groups, and individuals, vitamin D deficiency is relatively easy to contract. Much of the credit for the dramatic reduction in the number of cases of rickets in the 20th century, especially among children, goes to the widely-used process of adding vitamin D to milk and other food products. However, in some impoverished countries where this process is not used and where people receive insufficient doses of the vitamin from sunlight and fish, the incidence of rickets remains widespread.

Even in the developed countries, certain groups of people are more at risk for vitamin D deficiency and they should take daily supplements of the vitamin. For example, because only very small amounts of vitamin D occur in vegetables and fruits, people who follow strict vegetarian diets need such supplements. As Krause and Mahan point out, anyone who is regularly shielded from sunlight also needs supplements, as in the case of:

> persons living in smoggy, sunless areas; wearing clothes which cover the body; working at night and staying indoors as elderly persons may do. In these special cases a small daily supplement of vitamin D is believed desirable. . . . For women during pregnancy and lactation [milk production], adequate vitamin D is needed to promote efficient use of the increased calcium and phosphorus in the diet. The optimum amount of vitamin D is not known, but on the basis of available evidence 400 [international] units [each day] is recommended.

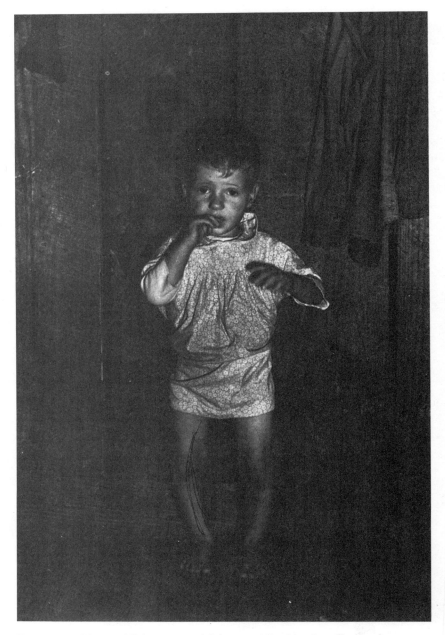

The bowed legs of this young child reveal that he is suffering from rickets, caused by a deficiency of vitamin D.

Some High Risk Groups

Just as vitamin D deficiency can be a higher risk for some groups than others, some other vitamin deficiencies affect mainly specific groups. For example, one type of vitamin B_{12} deficiency can occur when a person reduces or eliminates animal products, such as meat, seafood, eggs, milk, and butter, from the diet. Since these are the main sources of the vitamin, the person is at a higher risk for suffering a deficiency. Doctors refer to a serious deficiency of vitamin B_{12} as *pernicious anemia.* Symptoms include weakness, sore tongue, loss of weight, reduced oxygen content in the blood, and nervous disorders. Thus, it is best for those who wish to avoid animal products in their diets to take vitamin supplements containing vitamin B_{12}. It is important to note, however, that another type of deficiency of the vitamin results from an inability of the body to properly absorb the nutrient and, therefore, can affect a person in any group. In cases of both types of vitamin B_{12} deficiency, doctors often counteract the condition by administering several injections of the vitamin.

Another example of a specific group being more at risk for a vitamin deficiency is the case of vitamin K, also called quinones. Although some vitamin K is found in foods, such as green leafy vegetables, cabbage, cauliflower, egg yolk, and soybean oil, most of the body's supply of the vitamin is produced in the intestines. There, a special kind of bacteria that exists only in the body synthesizes vitamin K from various food nutrients. Most people get more than sufficient amounts of the vitamin from this process. The one group that does not benefit from the process is newborn infants. Apparently, their intestinal bacteria have not yet developed sufficiently to produce the vitamin and for a few days or longer after birth they are at high risk of suffering from a condition known as hemorrhagic disease of the newborn. This is characterized by abnormal bleeding and can be life-threatening. To avoid the problem, doctors recommend giving newborns one or two doses of vitamin K immediately after birth.

As already noted, most vitamin deficiency diseases are rare in developed countries like the United States. This is because of constant research in nutrition, widespread competent medical care, and increased awareness in many sectors of the public of the importance of a healthy diet. This last factor, awareness by individuals, is the most important key to avoiding such deficiencies. Each person should take responsibility for what he or she eats. This means learning about the RDA requirements of the various vitamins, finding out which foods are high or low in these nutrients, and adjusting food intake accordingly.

CHAPTER 4

MINERALS: LIFE'S VITAL BUILDING BLOCKS

A poster from the American Dietetic Association offers good advice on proper nutrition.

Minerals are *nonorganic,* or nonliving, chemical substances that are found in the ground and other natural locations. Plants take minerals from the soil and store them in their stems and leaves and, subsequently, animals take in the minerals by eating the plants. Like vitamins, minerals are essential to the body. However, in general minerals are needed in smaller amounts than vitamins. Also, scientists do not yet understand how and why minerals work in the body as well as they understand vitamins, and as a result the RDAs of many minerals are a bit less certain.

Scientists usually divide the minerals the body needs into two general groups—the *macrominerals* (or macronutrients) and the *microminerals* (or micronutrients). Most often, the macrominerals are those needed by the body in quantities of 100 milligrams or more a day, while the microminerals, sometimes referred to as "trace elements," are those measured in daily amounts of only a few milligrams or even by the *microgram,* one-millionth of a gram. The seven macrominerals are calcium, phosphorus, magnesium, sodium, potassium, chloride, and sulfur. Among the many microminerals the body needs are iron, copper, iodine, zinc, and flourine.

As in the case of individual vitamins, each mineral has its own specific function in the body. Yet most minerals have a few important functions in common. Among these are helping to regulate the body's water balance and maintaining the size and hardness of the bones. Minerals also aid in nerve function and muscle contractions, help control the balance of acidic substances in the body, and constitute vital components of essential body chemicals such as hormones and enzymes. In short, without the minerals, even the ones needed in the tiniest amounts, the body could not function properly.

Calcium and Phosphorus for Bones and Teeth

Calcium is the most abundant mineral found in the body, comprising about 39% of the body's mineral content and about 2% of the body's weight. Calcium is also one of the most important minerals utilized by the body because it is essential for the formation of bones and teeth. The bones store extra calcium, which the body can extract and use when too little calcium is being consumed. As Martha Davis Dunn explains:

About 99 percent of body calcium is present in bones and teeth. The remaining one percent is found in the soft tissues and body fluids. Calcium is stored in the bones as well. If the intake is not sufficient, calcium can be removed from the bones to meet other essential body needs. This may occur [in women] during pregnancy and lactation, when the calcium requirement of the body increases. The dentine and enamel of the teeth are more stable than and do not yield calcium [for other needs] as readily as the bones.

Calcium also exists in the blood, where the mineral helps in the formation of normal clots. In addition, calcium aids in nerve function, makes muscle contractions possible, and, along with other nutrients, helps regulate the heart beat.

Because calcium is stored in the bones for possible future use and utilized by the body in varying amounts and in several different ways, it is sometimes difficult to determine just how much of the mineral people need each day. Most studies in this area suggest that adults should take in about 800 milligrams of calcium per day. Children, whose bones are still forming, and pregnant women, who must supply calcium for their growing fetuses, should consume higher levels of the mineral, probably about 1.2 grams (1,200 milligrams) daily. Among the best food sources of calcium are milk, cheese, yogurt, sardines, turnip greens, collard greens, and broccoli. For instance, one cup of whole milk contains 291 milligrams of calcium, one ounce of Swiss cheese 272 milligrams, and one cup of cooked collard greens 357 milligrams. It is important to note, however, that no matter how much calcium the body takes in, most of it will be unusable without a simultaneous, adequate intake of vitamin D. As discussed earlier, this vitamin is essential to the normal absorption and utilization of the mineral.

Phosphorus is the second most abundant mineral found in the body, making up about 22% of the overall mineral content. About 80% of the body's phosphorus exists in the bones and teeth, while the remainder is distributed fairly evenly throughout the body's fluids and cells. In

Cheese and other dairy products are a good source of the mineral calcium, necessary for strong bones. Crackers and bread provide the mineral sodium.

addition to adding rigidity to the bones and teeth, phosphorus helps metabolize carbohydrates, fats, and proteins. The mineral also helps support nerve tissues and plays an important role in the normal functioning of enzymes. As in the case of calcium, phosphorus absorption is greatly increased in the presence of vitamin D. Usually, foods rich in protein and calcium also contain considerable amounts of phosphorus, among them: milk, cheese, meat, poultry, fish, eggs, grains, and nuts.

Iron for Healthy Blood

Iron is one of most abundant minerals in nature, making up a large proportion of the earth's core and considerable proportions of some rocks and soils. Proportionally, however, iron is much less abundant in the human body, constituting one of the microminerals. Nevertheless, the substance is absolutely essential to normal body structure and function. One of the major components of *hemoglobin,* the oxygen-bearing protein in the red blood cells, iron helps transport oxygen through the bloodstream to the tissues and cells. There, the hemoglobin releases the oxygen and carries carbon dioxide back through the bloodstream to the lungs. Red blood cells live for about 120 days. After these cells die, they release their iron, which is then recycled, becoming part of newly forming hemoglobin. Iron is also an important component of *myoglobin,* an oxygen-bearing substance in the muscles, and enzymes that metabolize sugars and fats.

Information about how iron is consumed by the body and about how much iron people need in their diets is still incomplete. However, some facts about iron intake have been established. According to Shils and Young:

> Most published figures, obtained from dietary surveys rather than actual analysis, indicate that the average daily intake is between 10 and 30 milligrams. The diets of people who live in Western countries contain about 5 to 7 milligrams of iron per 1,000 calories [of food consumed]. A weight-conscious young woman who limits her intake to 1,000 to 1,500 calories per day will therefore consume only 6 to 9 milligrams of food iron. . . . Other studies have shown that iron utensils contribute significantly to the iron content of cooked foods. The substitution of aluminum, stainless steel, or plastic-coated pots and pans has almost certainly had an adverse effect on dietary iron intake. . . . Failure to consider the iron content of drinking fluids introduces into dietary surveys another source of error that is of varying significance in different areas. Some ciders and wines may contain as much as 2 to 16 milligrams of iron or more per liter. . . . The iron content of city water supplies is usually low, but more than 5 milligrams per liter may be found in the water from some deep wells.

Because of these and other facts discovered in surveys, researchers have established the RDA of iron for adults at about 10 milligrams per day. Growing children and pregnant women need more iron, as do women undergoing menstruation, or having their periods, a process

Whole grain breads and cereals are a good source of iron.

during which iron is lost in the blood and tissue expelled from the body. The RDA of iron for these groups is about 18 milligrams a day. Some of the best food sources of iron are meat, fish, eggs, dried fruits, nuts, whole grains, green leafy vegetables, and raisins. Three ounces of ground beef contains 3 milligrams of iron, one medium egg 1 milligram, one-half cup of oysters 6.6 milligrams, one cup of oatmeal 1.4 milligrams, and one cup of raisins 5.1 milligrams.

Sodium and Potassium and the Body's Fluids

Sodium and potassium are also minerals essential to normal body function. Sodium is the main component of the body's extracellular fluids, those fluids that occur outside of the cells. By contrast, potassium is a major element in the intracellular fluid, the fluid inside the cells.

Sodium's main function is to regulate the body's acid balance, that is, to make sure that the fluids of the body do not contain too much or too little acid. The mineral also plays a role in regulating both the volume of fluids in the body and the blood pressure.

The amount of sodium needed by the body varies according to the person and his or her activity level. People engaged in an average amount of physical activity generally take in much more sodium than they need and excrete about 90% of it in the urine. On the other hand, those individuals who perform very strenuous jobs or who exercise both regularly and vigorously tend to lose a great deal of sodium in their sweat. Also, sick people who undergo vomiting or diarrhea lose considerable amounts of sodium. Thus, it is not always easy to know how much sodium must be consumed. Another complication is that ordinary table salt, which contains 40% sodium, is used as a preservative and flavor-enhancing additive in many foods, and as a result many people may consume too much sodium. In her book *Culinary Nutrition for Foodservice Professionals,* Carol A. Hodges states that salt:

> is liberally sprinkled into foods both during cooking
> and eating to enhance flavor. The problem is that
> people consume too much and high intakes have been
> linked to hypertension (high blood pressure) which in
> turn can increase the risk of heart and kidney disease,
> and strokes. Only about 20 percent of the population
> is sodium sensitive, or reactive to even small amounts
> of it, but there is no way to tell who is and who is not
> until problems begin to appear. Since studies have

shown that population groups with a high incidence of hypertension also consume a lot of sodium, recommendations for intake have been established at a maximum of 3,000 milligrams per day, slightly more than 1 teaspoon of salt. Most people consume three or more times this amount.

While the maximum amount of sodium that should be consumed is 3,000 milligrams per day, many health experts advise taking in an amount closer to the minimum that scientists estimate is safe—about 1,100 milligrams per day. This means avoiding the use of extra salt as an additive and reducing the consumption of processed foods high in sodium, such as crackers, bacon, and bread. Good natural sources of

Dietitians working with school lunch programs must ensure that the children receive adequate amounts of vitamins and minerals.

sodium are cheese, milk, shellfish, poultry, eggs, unprocessed cereals, and fruits and vegetables.

Potassium makes up about 5% of the mineral content of the body. Potassium is chemically similar to sodium, and like sodium it is involved in maintaining the body's acid and fluid balances. Another important function of potassium is helping the nerves and muscles work together to produce normal muscle contractions. Fairly high levels of the mineral are found in meat, milk, citrus fruit, bananas, apricots, broccoli, spinach, tomatoes, dark green leafy vegetables, and cereals. In fact, potassium is so widely distributed in foods that deficiencies are extremely rare and no definite RDA requirements have been set.

Other Essential Minerals

Some of the other minerals essential to good health are chloride, copper, iodine, magnesium, and zinc. Chloride, a macromineral, is an important component of the gastric juice used in digestion. Chloride is also necessary for proper absorption of vitamin B_{12} and iron, still another example of how vitamins and minerals work together to make the body work properly. Like sodium, chloride is easily lost through excessive sweating. But chloride is just as easily replaced, since it is a major component of table salt, which, as pointed out earlier, most people consume in generous quantities. Although normal salt intake provides all the chloride the body needs, the mineral is also found in milk, meat, and eggs.

Copper is a micromineral, the exact functions of which are still not precisely understood. Scientists are sure, however, that copper helps prevent anemia and aids in the development and maintenance of bone, nerves, and connective tissues. Copper concentrations are highest in the brain, liver, heart, kidneys, and bones. The RDA of copper for adults is about 2 to 3 milligrams, an amount easily obtainable from foods, the richest sources being shellfish, liver, kidney, nuts, and raisins.

Iodine, another micromineral, is essential to the body because it affects the workings of the thyroid gland, the gland that produces an important hormone that regulates metabolism. About one-third of the

Long-grain rice seeds. Most of the vitamins and minerals in rice are in the husks, so if the husks are removed, as with polished rice, much of the nutritional value is lost.

iodine consumed by the average person goes into the production of the thyroid hormone. The rest of the iodine is excreted in the urine. The two best dietary sources of the mineral are seafood, including clams, oysters, lobsters, sardines, and many fish, and table salt that has been *iodized,* or had iodine added to it. Because only about half of the salt used in the United States is iodized, many health officials worry that some people, especially those who eat little or no seafood, may not be getting enough iodine in their diets. Therefore, it may be important for consumers to make sure they buy iodized salt.

The macromineral magnesium exists in the body in the form of magnesium salts. About 60% of the body's magnesium is found in the bones, 26% in the muscles, and the remainder in the soft tissues and fluids. Magnesium helps various bodily chemical reactions take place. The mineral also aids in the regulation of body temperature and the synthesis of protein in tissues. Magnesium often plays an antagonistic, or opposing, role to that of calcium in bodily functions. For example, while calcium acts as a stimulator of muscle contractions, magnesium acts as a muscle relaxer. Whole grains, nuts, yeast, cocoa, and leafy vegetables are excellent sources of magnesium, while meat, milk, and seafood provide smaller amounts of the mineral.

Zinc, a micromineral, is an important component of at least 70 of the enzymes used in metabolism. Zinc is also found in red blood cells and helps promote normal growth, prevent anemia, and repair wounds. The RDA of zinc is about 15 milligrams daily, although pregnant and lactating women should add another 5 to 10 milligrams more per day. Rich sources of zinc include meat, seafood, poultry, eggs, whole wheat or rye breads, wheat germ, and nuts.

Some of the other minerals utilized in varying amounts by the body include sulfur, manganese, selenium, molybdenum, chromium, cobalt, and flourine. While the roles played by some of these in maintaining life and health are fairly well understood, others are still being studied to determine exactly how they function. As this kind of research continues, scientists are constantly shedding new light on both vitamins and minerals and the complex ways they act and interact in the human body.

CHAPTER 5

MINERAL DEFICIENCIES

STAND TALL

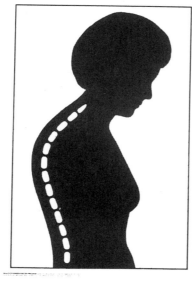

in the years to come

Fight osteoporosis, the bone-thinning disease that occurs with age. Exercise and eat calcium-rich foods.

Before beginning an exercise program or changing your diet, be sure to consult your physician.

This poster warns about the dangers of osteoporosis, the weakening of bone structure, that often occurs later in life if there is insufficient calcium in the diet.

Mineral deficiencies, like vitamin deficiencies, have come to be understood only in the last two centuries. Although many societies through the ages found reliable ways to treat some mineral deficiencies, as in the case of the early Chinese prescribing consumption of seaweed to cure goiter, people had no idea what caused these conditions in the first place or why the treatments worked. Systematic research and experimentation in the early years of the 20th century cleared up many of these mysteries. Yet a considerable amount of information about minerals and their associated deficiencies remained sketchy a lot longer and facts about some minerals are still unclear. Zinc deficiency, for example, was fully described and understood as late as the 1960s. And the bodily functions and deficiencies of minute trace minerals such as nickel and tin remain poorly understood in the 1990s. Scientists agree, however, that it is only a matter of time before research reveals a complete picture of minerals, including how deficiencies of these substances occur.

From Cavities to Weakened Bones

Lack of calcium in the diet is one of the better-understood mineral deficiencies. Calcium deficiencies remain fairly common, even in developed countries, and symptoms and effects vary widely in their nature and severity. According to Krause and Mahan:

> A moderate degree of calcium deficiency is believed to be quite prevalent during pregnancy, and also in childhood; it is usually much worse during adolescence. During the adolescent period the requirement [for calcium] is increased while in contrast too often the intake of calcium-rich foods is decreased. The desire to remain slim is a factor, especially among girls. It is during the adolescent period that dental caries [cavities] tend to become prevalent, a condition believed to depend on nutritional status and calcium metabolism.

This means that many children, though consuming sufficient amounts of calcium through milk and other foods, may be lacking adequate vitamin D in their diets and, therefore, may not be metabolizing enough of the calcium. Luckily, for most people the effects of this moderate form of calcium deficiency are relatively mild.

More acute or prolonged lack of calcium, however, can be considerably more severe. Although rickets is primarily caused by a lack of vitamin D, the two nutrients and their functions are so closely interrelated that a lack of calcium can also cause the disease. This happens mainly in children, most commonly in poor countries where malnutrition is a big problem. Side effects include stunted growth and poorly developed bones and teeth.

Lack of calcium is also a problem for adults, especially after the age of 50. Large numbers of older people, in both developed and underdeveloped countries, suffer from a condition known as *osteoporosis,* a reduction in the amount of bone tissues, resulting in a general weakening of the skeleton. In such cases, the less calcium consumed and absorbed by the body, the weaker the bones become. People with osteoporosis have an increased risk of bone fractures, even from minor falls. The condition is widespread, affecting millions of people, but is more prevalent in older women than older men by a factor of four to one.

It is important to note that calcium deficiency is not the only factor that contributes to osteoporosis. Normal hormonal and other physical changes that come with increasing age apparently also play a part, as does inactivity and the intake of vitamin D. Therefore, avoiding or lessening the effects of osteoporosis must involve not only making sure one takes in enough calcium, but also monitoring and, when necessary, increasing vitamin D intake, and also engaging in regular exercise well into old age. Regarding the latter, several recent studies have shown that moderate, supervised weight lifting by seniors, even in their 70s and 80s, helps keep the bones, as well as the muscles, ligaments, and tendons, strong and healthy. This both reduces one's risks of osteoporosis and related injuries and increases the number of one's active, useful years. Seniors worried about osteoporosis should consult their doctor before taking vitamin and mineral supplements or beginning a vigorous exercise program.

Iron Deficiency—Past and Present

Lack of iron is perhaps the most common of the nutrient deficiencies. It is very common in infants, especially premature babies, because at birth the body possesses little stored iron, and also because milk, the

The propensity of children to eat candy and junk food may result in
vitamin and mineral deficiencies.

main diet of infants, has a low iron content. Lack of iron is less common but still a problem in older children. Studies indicate that 5% to 7% of children aged four to eight in the United States suffer from *iron deficiency anemia,* a lack of sufficient iron in the blood. Symptoms include weakness, fatigue, headache, and shortness of breath. Other studies suggest that 35% to 58% of young, otherwise healthy women in the United States may suffer from some degree of anemia due to insufficient iron. Martha Dunn states that "iron deficiency anemia is a significant medical and health problem, causing few deaths but contributing seriously to the weakness, ill health, and substandard performance of millions of people." And according to the World Health Organization, or WHO, iron deficiency is a serious problem affecting large segments of the populations in 30% to 50% of the underdeveloped countries.

Evidence indicates that iron deficiency is not a new problem. Lack of the proper amount of dietary iron was apparently widespread in many societies through the ages. Shils and Young explain that archaeological studies of:

> the ancient inhabitants of the southwestern United States indicate that severe iron deficiency may have been prevalent among sedentary [non-migrating] agricultural people of the canyon bottomlands, who depended upon maize [corn] as their nearly sole dietary resource. Maize is poor in iron. . . . Skeletons excavated in such areas reveal marked bony deformities and spongy porosity [pockmarks] of the skull . . . attributed to extreme iron impoverishment. . . . [By contrast] the people of the Aztec and Maya cultures of meso-America, where maize was the major food, do not appear to have been afflicted with this disorder, perhaps because they also consumed beans rich in iron.

The prevalence of iron deficiency in both the past and present suggests that governments should do more to educate their citizens about iron consumption and also that many individuals need to monitor their iron intake more carefully.

The problem of iron deficiency anemia is complicated by the fact that other factors besides insufficient dietary intake of iron can cause the condition. In fact, it is quite possible to consume more than adequate amounts of the mineral and still develop anemia. For example, if the iron taken in is poorly absorbed, perhaps because of a lack of vitamin C, little of the mineral will reach the bloodstream. Blood loss is another cause of anemia. People who suffer from bleeding hemorrhoids or ulcers, frequent nosebleeds, other kinds of internal bleeding, or intestinal parasites that live on blood tend to lose considerable amounts of iron, and this can sometimes lead to anemia. Women who experience frequent, heavy menstruation or who have several closely spaced pregnancies, both of which tend to deplete the body's

A deficiency of the mineral iron can be a contributing factor to baldness.

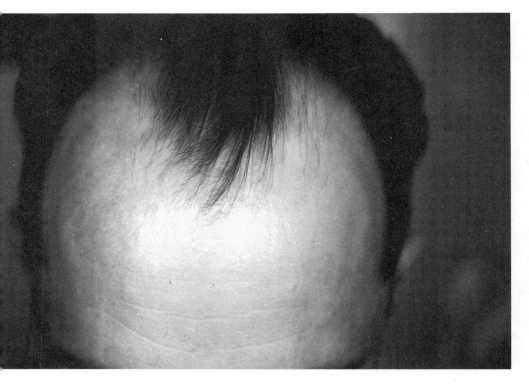

stores of iron, are also candidates for anemia. People in these groups should take dietary iron supplements to make up for their losses of this important mineral.

Because women are so often at risk for iron deficiency anemia, the book *The New Our Bodies, Ourselves,* compiled by the Boston Women's Health Book Collective, advises women who must take iron supplements that:

> They work best on an empty stomach, but if they cause nausea or cramps take them with food. Taking vitamin C at the same time will increase absorption. Even so, some women find . . . that they cannot absorb iron pills. Eating blackstrap molasses has helped some women. Iron pills can cause tarry stools or constipation, which can be remedied by eating more whole grains, bran and fruit and drinking lots of water. Iron interferes with the absorption of vitamin E. If you are taking vitamin E supplements, be sure to take them at least six hours before the iron.

Other Mineral Deficiencies

As mentioned earlier, iodine deficiency can lead to a condition known as goiter, an enlargement of the thyroid gland. This can be painful and dangerous in severe cases when the enlarged gland presses on the wind pipe and esophagus, impeding breathing and swallowing. Goiter is most common in areas with iodine-poor soil, including the European Alps, the Himalaya mountains, the Thames valley in England, much of Central America, and the Great Lakes Basin in the United States, once referred to as the goiter belt because of the high incidence of the condition in the region. Once iodized salt came into common use in the 20th century, the number of cases of goiter dropped sharply in the goiter belt. However, the condition remains widespread in many areas of the world. According to WHO, between 200 and 300 million people worldwide suffer from goiter as a result of iodine deficiency.

Not surprisingly, the best way to counteract iodine deficiency is to increase one's intake of iodine. This can be done, as already explained,

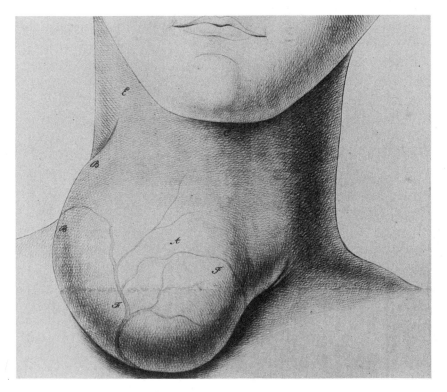

A 19th-century sketch of a person suffering from goiter, an inflammation of the endocrine glands caused by a deficiency of iodine.

by eating seafoods, as well as fruits and vegetables grown in iodine-rich soil. In some instances, people living in areas with iodine-poor soil can benefit from fruits, vegetables, beverages, and fertilizers trucked in from other areas. However, to be on the safe side these people should be sure to use iodized salt.

Magnesium deficiency, which bears the tongue-twisting medical name of hypomagneamic tetany syndrome deficiency, usually develops during the onset of certain diseases and adverse physical conditions, among them renal disease, a kidney ailment; hyperthyroidism, a condition in which the thyroid gland speeds up the metabolism; intestinal malabsorption, the inability of the body to absorb certain nutrients; acute alcoholism; diabetes, a condition characterized by high blood sugar; and postsurgical stress. All of these conditions result in either a decreased intake or an increased loss of magnesium. For example, an acute alcoholic substitutes alcohol for many healthy foods and thereby does not take in enough of the mineral. And a person with intestinal malabsorption is unable to utilize most of the magnesium he

A poster from the American Cancer Society explains that a balanced diet may help to avoid cancer.

A defense against cancer can be cooked up in your kitchen.

There is evidence that diet and cancer are related. Follow these modifications in your daily diet to reduce chances of getting cancer:

1. Eat more high-fiber foods such as fruits and vegetables and whole-grain cereals.

2. Include dark green and deep yellow fruits and vegetables rich in vitamins A and C.

3. Include cabbage, broccoli, brussels sprouts, kohlrabi and cauliflower.

4. Be moderate in consumption of salt-cured, smoked, and nitrite-cured foods.

5. Cut down on total fat intake from animal sources and fats and oils.

6. Avoid obesity.

7. Be moderate in consumption of alcoholic beverages.

No one faces cancer alone.   **♦ AMERICAN ♀ CANCER ♥ SOCIETY**

Health stores selling various preparations of vitamins and minerals are quite common today, but the consumer must make certain that these preparations are safe and do not make exaggerated health claims. Most vitamins and minerals shoud come from a well-balanced diet.

or she does consume and therefore loses most supplies of the mineral by excretion. The symptoms of magnesium deficiency are depression, muscular weakness, vertigo, or severe dizziness, and tremors and convulsions. This deficiency is rare in developed countries but more prevalent in impoverished nations where disease and ill health are more

widespread. In most cases, injections with the chemical magnesium sulfate provide prompt relief from the condition.

Zinc deficiency can be serious and even life-threatening in some instances. Symptoms are: stunted growth resulting in abnormally short stature, underdevelopment of the genitals, anemia, delayed wound healing, and hypogeusia, or decreased sensitivity of the taste buds. A deficiency of zinc occurs either through lack of the mineral in the diet or as a result of the body's inability to absorb it properly. Researcher K. M. Hambidge performed a study in the early 1970s of diet-related zinc deficiency in the United States. According to Krause and Mahan:

> Hambidge performed zinc analyses on hair in 338 middle and upper class children and adults in Denver, Colorado. He found ten children with very low hair zinc levels (less than 70 parts per million). Most of these children also had a history of poor appetite, were below the tenth percentile for height [shorter than at least 90% of their classmates] and had hypogeusia. All of these conditions improved upon administration of zinc sulfate. The diets of these children had consisted of very little meat and a great deal of milk, a poor source of zinc.

This and other studies of dietary zinc suggest that while severe zinc deficiency is rare in the United States, milder cases may be more prevalent than doctors previously realized. In a 1973 article in the *American Journal of Clinical Nutrition,* researcher H. Sandstead suggested that a large proportion of the population, especially low-income people whose diets are nutritionally inadequate, may suffer from a "marginal zinc intake." It is important, therefore, to make sure that at least some zinc-rich foods, such as meats, poultry, wheat products, and nuts, are a part of one's diet.

The serious consequences of zinc deficiency and the ease with which they can be avoided by eating a balanced diet provide a lesson that applies to all of the dietary minerals, and the vitamins as well. In short, learning the facts about nutrition and applying them to one's own food intake will greatly reduce the chances of experiencing health problems caused by nutritional deficiencies.

CHAPTER 6

OVERDOING
IT

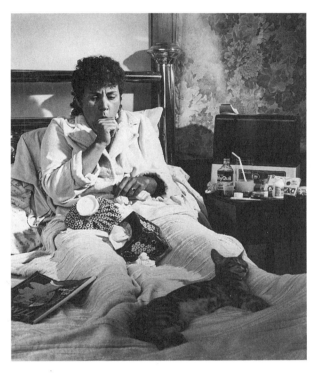

People with common colds often take massive doses of vitamin C, but there is no conclusive evidence that it can shorten the duration of such illnesses.

Just as taking in inadequate quantities of vitamins and minerals can be unhealthy, consuming these nutrients in unusually high doses can also produce adverse physical effects. Because consuming too much of certain nutrients can be *toxic,* or poisonous, to the body, doctors refer to the condition brought on by such overdoses as *toxicity.*

Some vitamins and minerals are more toxic than others. And each has its own individual safe level of intake. On the other hand, some minerals that are nonessential to the body, such as mercury, are potentially dangerous when consumed because they can produce toxicity in relatively minor doses. Rising environmental levels of these substances represent a real health threat in many areas.

Also, there is still considerable disagreement in the medical community about the possible benefits of taking higher-than-normal doses of certain vitamins. For instance, some doctors and researchers believe that megadoses of vitamin C produce a variety of positive health effects. Others say that some of these claims are false or exaggerated. In the cases of most vitamins and minerals, however, there is little or no dispute among scientists. These essential nutrients are good when taken in the right quantities, they say, but, as in other aspects of life, too much of a good thing can be detrimental.

Toxic Effects of Vitamins

Too much vitamin A, for example, is certainly detrimental to health. Vitamin A toxicity, or hypervitaminosis A, can result from intake of several times the RDA for the nutrient. The condition takes two forms: acute, caused by one or two sudden overdoses of the vitamin, and chronic, caused by regular, prolonged overdoses. Acute vitamin A toxicity, most often seen in children, causes such effects as nausea, vomiting, headache, vertigo, and blurred or double vision. When the dose is very large, the victim may also suffer from drowsiness, reduced physical activity, skin eruptions, and in the most extreme cases coma, convulsions, and finally death.

Chronic vitamin A toxicity results from consuming amounts of 10 or more times the RDA for the vitamin for an extended period, usually several weeks or months. According to Krause and Mahan, this condition:

> has been noted to stunt growth [in children] or has left one leg two or three inches shorter than the other. The difference in leg length usually develops because the

A program organized by the Department of Agriculture provides pregnant mothers with nutritious foods designed to keep their babies healthy.

child tends to favor whichever leg becomes more painful. Transient hydrocephalus [increased water pressure on the brain] and vomiting are the prominent symptoms in children receiving overdoses of vitamin A. Bone fragility, thickening of long bones and deep bone pain, loss of appetite, coarsening and loss of hair, scaly skin eruptions, enlargement of the liver and spleen, irritability, double vision and skin rashes are among the symptoms of prolonged, excessive intake.

Although such extreme cases of vitamin A toxicity are relatively rare, milder cases of chronic toxicity are fairly common among adolescents who take high doses of the vitamin for treatment of the skin condition acne. Often, these young people experience some of the uncomfortable symptoms of toxicity without realizing the cause, especially if they do not report these symptoms to their doctors. In most of these cases, lowering the consumption of the vitamin to normal levels eliminates the symptoms within a few days.

Vitamin D toxicity, or hypervitaminosis D, results when a person consumes many times the RDA for the vitamin for an extended period of time. Unlike the case of vitamin A, one or two overdoses of vitamin D produce no discernible ill effects. In general, the effects of vitamin D toxicity are an exaggeration of the normal functions of the nutrient. In other words, since a normal amount of the vitamin keeps the bones healthy by helping the body absorb calcium, too much vitamin D leads to excessive calcification of the bones. Other symptoms of the condition are the development of kidney stones, headache, nausea, and diarrhea. Babies inadvertently given too much vitamin D suffer from intestinal upsets, buildup of calcium deposits in the soft tissues, retarded growth, and mental retardation. Vitamin D toxicity can also cause *hypercalcemia,* or excess calcium in the blood. All of these problems, if recognized early, can be successfully treated by reducing intake of the vitamin.

In general, the water-soluble vitamins have no known toxic effects. This is mainly because the body does not store these substances in large quantities and, therefore, excessive amounts tend to pass harmlessly out of the body in the urine. However, large doses of some of these vitamins can produce discomfort. High levels of niacin in the body, for example, can cause temporary side effects such as tingling sensations, flushing of the skin, and a throbbing sensation in the head. And too much vitamin B_6 can cause drowsiness.

Vitamin C and the Benefits of Vitamin Supplements

Vitamin C, another water-soluble vitamin, also produces a few unpleasant side effects when taken in unusually large quantities. In some people, megadoses of the vitamin, in the range of 1,000 to 3,000 milligrams per day, have caused diarrhea and irritation of the urinary tract. However, many people have taken large doses of vitamin C without apparent side effects. Perhaps this is because the body becomes saturated with the nutrient at levels of 100 to 1,000 milligrams, depending upon the person, and then automatically excretes the rest.

Vitamin C is a very controversial nutrient. This is because there is a lot of argument among researchers about whether large doses of the vitamin are useless or perhaps even harmful, or whether such doses may provide special health benefits. The controversy began in 1970 when Nobel Prize winner Dr. Linus Pauling published his book *Vitamin C and the Common Cold.* Pauling maintained that megadoses of the vitamin can help protect the body against the common cold. While sales of vitamin C skyrocketed in the United States and many other countries, many scientists disputed Pauling's claims. They insisted that the vitamin does not ward off colds and that encouraging the consumption of huge doses might at best raise false hopes and cause people to waste their money, and at worst produce adverse health effects. A number of studies of high vitamin C intake have been conducted since that time. Some seemed to indicate that, while it does not prevent someone from catching a cold, the vitamin might reduce the severity and duration of many cold symptoms. Other studies have produced inconclusive results, and arguments on the subject continue in the medical community.

By contrast, more conclusive evidence has recently convinced many doctors and researchers that large regular doses of vitamin C, as in the case of vitamin E discussed earlier, may help eliminate the effects of oxidation in the body. This may reduce the risk of certain diseases and conditions doctors suspect are either caused or worsened by oxidation. In a June 1993 issue of *Newsweek,* science writer Geoffrey Cowley summarized the findings of 20 recent studies that considered the effects of vitamin C intake on the incidence of mouth, throat, and stomach cancers. "In 18 of those 20 studies," Cowley reported, "low intake [of the vitamin] emerged as a risk factor: on average, people consuming the least vitamin C were stricken at twice the rate of those consuming the most." Similar results have come from studies of the relationship between vitamin C and heart disease. In 1992, researchers at UCLA announced the results of a decade-long federal health survey which showed, among other things, that extra vitamin C taken regularly may reduce the risk of death by heart attacks. In the study, men who consumed 300 milligrams of the vitamin daily, or about five times the RDA, had 40% fewer deaths than those consuming the RDA.

This suggests that taking supplements that contain larger than normal amounts of certain vitamins may be beneficial to health. In addition to the promising evidence surrounding vitamins E and C, separate evidence exists showing positive health effects for beta carotene, one of the provitamin A carotenes. According to Cowley:

> Regina Ziegler, an epidemiologist [doctor who studies the incidence and spread of disease] at the National Cancer Institute . . . analyzed more than 20 studies that tracked cancers of the lung and other tissues in relation to beta carotene intake. Virtually all the studies linked high levels of the nutrient to low rates of lung cancer. The studies showed similar but less dramatic patterns for cancers of the mouth, throat, stomach, bladder and rectum. . . . Meanwhile, researchers at Harvard have found preliminary evidence that 50-milligram beta carotene supplements, taken every other day, can halve the risk of heart attack among men with histories of cardiovascular disease.

All of this heartening evidence does not prove that vitamin supplements are miracle drugs that will guarantee a life free of serious

It is important to know what is in dietary supplements and what health claims they make. This 19th-century preparation makes health claims that would be forbidden by law today.

disease. Nor is taking such supplements necessarily the best way to stay healthy. As nearly all doctors advocate, a balanced diet, regular exercise, and the avoidance of smoking and heavy drinking are the most effective means of achieving and maintaining good health. But many doctors now say that reducing the risks of cancer, heart disease, and other health problems by consuming safe vitamin supplements is an extra precaution worth taking. And, as Cowley says, "this medical revolution won't require a new generation of weaponry. Your corner drugstore is already armed to the teeth."

Mineral Toxicity

In general, excessively large doses of minerals are more toxic and have more dangerous side effects than correspondingly large doses of vitamins. Doctors recognize two kinds of mineral toxicity: poisoning by consumption of excessive amounts of minerals which are essential to the body, and poisoning resulting from the body's contamination by nonessential minerals.

Iron is one of the essential minerals that can be dangerous if consumed in large amounts. Iron toxicity, sometimes referred to as iron overload, can cause a number of harmful conditions. Most of these are characterized by symptoms such as cirrhosis, or scarring, of the liver; diabetes; and changes in skin *pigmentation,* or coloring. Shils and Young describe one example of iron overload known as Bantu Siderosis, saying:

> iron overload in blacks of South Africa (first recognized in those of the Bantu linguistic stock, although not limited or predetermined by language) results from long-continued exposure to diets containing too much iron, derived largely from cooking pots and from the steel barrels used in the preparation of fermented alcoholic beverages. In adult males, the intake may exceed 100 milligrams [of] iron per day . . . and is usually more severe in males because their alcoholic consumption tends to be greater. . . . Approximately 20 percent of these subjects develop clinical diabetes.

Meat can be an important source of B-complex vitamins and protein, but it is high in fat, which is unhealthy.

Excessive amounts of copper, another of the essential minerals, can lead to a condition known as Wilson's disease. It is characterized by slow but steady cell damage, pigmentation changes in the skin, the development of excess fibrous, or coarse, tissue in various areas of the body, and nerve damage. Although Wilson's disease is relatively un-

A poster advises pregnant woman on how to protect their unborn babies from iron deficiency.

common, milder forms of copper poisoning may be much more prevalent, with the victims suffering from a range of uncomfortable side effects and having no idea why. This is probably because of the widespread use of copper pipes and utensils in developed countries. Like iron overload, copper toxicity can result from eating or drinking foods that have come into contact with surfaces containing the mineral. In his work, *The Complete Book of Minerals for Health,* nutrition expert J. I. Rodale offers the warning:

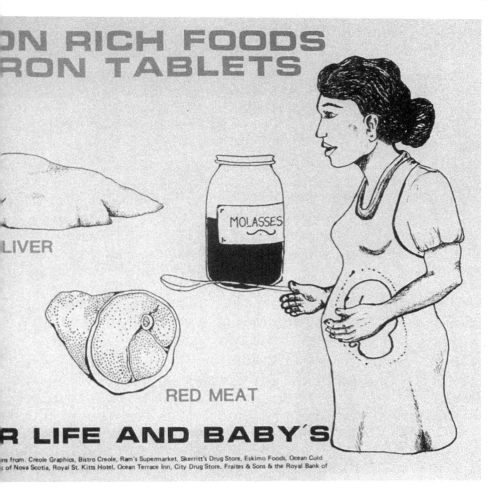

ON RICH FOODS
RON TABLETS

LIVER

MOLASSES

RED MEAT

R LIFE AND BABY'S

It is generally well-known that copper contaminates liquids or foods with which it comes in contact. It seems to us that alcoholic beverages would be even more subject to contamination than other things. So it was difficult for us to believe that [beer] brewers used copper in their breweries. What was our surprise, then, to find in a brewery magazine a double-page ad for copper piping and copper brew kettles with the slogan "Copper brews beer best." If you must drink beer, at least do make an effort to find out whether your brand is made in copper brewery equipment. Write to the manufacturers and ask them. . . . In choosing foods, where there is the slightest doubt in your mind, don't take a chance on anything that may be contaminated with copper. . . . This warning holds good for your kitchen utensils as well. Copper utensils are beautiful to look at. . . . Keep them on the shelves and admire their beauty, but under no circumstances use them in any way where they will come in contact with food!

Unfortunately, some nonessential minerals sometimes make their way into people's bodies, causing a wide range of symptoms and side effects and occasionally even death. Lead poisoning is a prime example. It develops from a number of sources, among them leaded paint eaten by young children, pitchers, cups, and utensils painted with lead-based glaze, emissions from leaded gasoline floating in the air, higher-than-normal concentrations of lead in tobacco smoke, and lead pipes used in breweries and bottling plants. The early symptoms of lead poisoning are vomiting, irritability, loss of weight, weakness, headache, insomnia, or the inability to sleep, and anorexia. If the poisoning continues, anemia, blindness, mental retardation and other brain damage, and eventually death can result.

Interestingly, doctors have reported a sharp rise in cases of lead poisoning during the summer months. The current accepted explanation for this is that people are exposed to more sunlight in the summer. Vitamin D, which the body derives from sunlight, causes an increased dietary absorption of lead.

Mercury is another dangerous mineral poison. Excessive amounts of mercury can cause loss of vision, hearing, and coordination, as well as damage to the brain and other parts of the nervous system, all permanent effects. The body takes at least 70 days to flush out only half of the original mercury taken in. Scientists believe that the major source of mercury poisoning is the dumping of industrial wastes containing the mineral into the environment. Fish and other animals then consume the mercury and pass it up the food chain to humans. Public awareness of this danger increased abruptly after 77 people died from eating mercury-contaminated fish in Japan in 1961. After it was

ANTI-FAT

The Great Remedy for Corpulence

ALLAN'S ANTI-FAT

is composed of purely vegetable ingredients,
and is perfectly harmless. It acts upon the
food in the stomach, preventing its being converted into fat. Taken in accordance with
directions, **it will reduce a fat person
from two to five pounds per week.**

*Weight-reducing products have always been notorious for
exaggerated and inaccurate health claims, as shown in
this advertisement for a 19th-century diet preparation.*

proven that a nearby Japanese chemical company had caused the problem by dumping industrial wastes into the ocean, the company paid damages to the victims' families. Other similar cases of mercury poisoning have surfaced over the years. However, most health officials believe that these are still mainly isolated incidents. As far as can be determined, although most of the fish eaten around the world does contain traces of mercury, these traces are too small to constitute a health hazard unless, as Rodale asserts, "such fish are eaten to a ridiculous excess." Rodale goes on to advise anyone worried about the dangers of mercury in fish that:

> The best way to avoid contact with organic mercury in fish is to avoid fish—as well as water—from inland lakes and streams that may have been polluted by . . . mercury dumping. Pass up large predatory fish, which eat smaller fish and may accumulate any excess mercury through the food chain, in favor of smaller ones, or best yet those species of fish which do not feed on other fish.

Thus, exercising caution is apparently the best way to avoid trouble. And this advice also applies to the cases of any other minerals which might cause poisoning when consumed in excess.

CHAPTER 7

THE RIGHT BALANCE: EATING A HEALTHY DIET

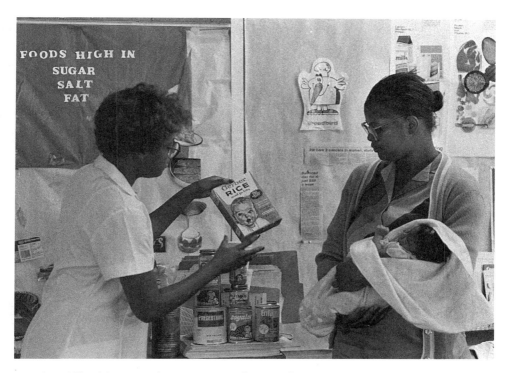

A nutritionist counsels a young mother on the proper foods for her baby's healthy growth.

When considering one's overall diet, consumption of vitamins and minerals should not be viewed as a separate issue. The physical effects of these nutrients are closely interrelated with the effects of other important nutritional factors, including food storage and preparation; proper consumption of carbohydrates, fats, and proteins, which may be referred to as *large macronutrients;* physical activity and exercise; the intake of harmful substances such as environmental toxins, tobacco smoke, and alcohol and other drugs; and the widespread occurrence of destructive eating disorders such as *bulimia* and anorexia. All of these factors have some kind of bearing, either direct or indirect, on how vitamins and minerals are absorbed and utilized in the body. Therefore, in order to understand the big picture of a healthy

The proper preparation of food is also very important, to ensure that dangerous microorganisms are destroyed while the nutritional content of the food is not degraded.

diet in which vitamins and minerals play an integral part, it is important to consider these other factors.

Vitamin Loss in Food Storage and Preparation

Regarding food storage and preparation, a general rule of thumb is that the longer foods are stored, the more nutritive value they lose. This is

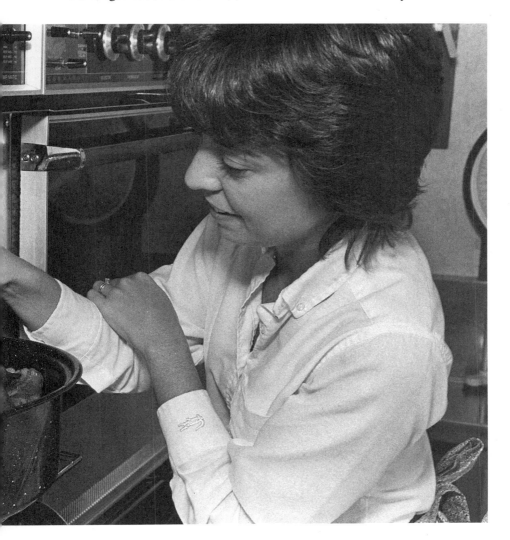

because most foods can be depleted of measurable amounts of vitamin and mineral content, especially water-soluble vitamin content, by prolonged contact with air, sunlight, and heat. This is why vegetables and fruits stay fresher and more nutritious longer when stored in bins in a dark, cold refrigerator. An exception to this rule is the canning process. According to nutrition expert Benjamin T. Burton:

> Today, canning results in minimal nutritive losses. . . . The vitamin content of canned foods reflects the variations in the nutrient values of the raw materials used, along with the methods employed in preparation and processing. Exposure to air (oxygen), contact with hot water, and heating . . . are responsible for reductions in vitamin content which may occur during canning. However, with up-to-date equipment and methods, the vitamins contained in the raw foods are retained to a high degree in the canned product.

Nutritive losses during prolonged storage of canned foods are generally minimal and due mainly to temperature differences. For example, when stored at 80°F for one year, food will lose about 15% to 30% of its vitamin C. At 65°F, the loss is only 5% to 15%, and as the temperature continues to drop so does the percentage of vitamin loss. Losses of thiamine are similar to those of vitamin C, while losses of niacin, riboflavin, and the carotenes are markedly lower at the same temperatures. Freezing foods at 0°F, as might be expected, reduces nutritive loss to almost zero.

The processing of fresh foods in the kitchen, including trimming, washing, and cooking, reduces the nutritive values of the foods to some degree. Benjamin Burton explains:

> No matter how carefully washing and cooking are performed, loss of water soluble . . . or oxidation prone [nutrients] is inevitable. Similar to the situation in canning, losses in carotene, riboflavin, and niacin are not significant, though riboflavin may be destroyed by exposure to strong light. The final vitamin content of the finished food and the losses of thiamine and ascorbic acid [vitamin C] due to oxidation and heating

depend on the original freshness and vitamin content of the produce . . . and the cooking habits of the cook. . . . Cooking in a covered pot and the briefer cooking period associated with pressure cooking tend to preserve thiamine and ascorbic acid [as well as other nutrients].

The Difficulties of Choosing a Balanced Diet

As stressed earlier, getting the right amounts of vitamins and minerals in one's diet depends in large measure on consuming a balanced intake of different kinds of nutritious foods. Eating the proper daily proportions of the large macronutrients—carbohydrates, proteins, and fats—will, in most instances, ensure intake of the needed vitamins and minerals. Each of these large macronutrients contains or stores vitamins and minerals in varying amounts. According to nutritionists, the ideal daily dietary proportions of the large macronutrients are 50% carbohydrates, 15% proteins, and 35% fats.

These are general figures that apply to average people engaged in normal, moderate physical activity and allowances should be made for those people who are more active. For example, people who are constantly on the go may need a slightly higher percentage of carbohydrates for extra energy. Athletes need plenty of carbohydrates for the same reason. They should choose carbohydrate foods with naturally occurring sugars such as fructose rather than processed sugars, which have no nutritional value and are harder to digest. Among these foods are fruits, fruit juices, and vegetables. In addition, they should eat plenty of complex carbohydrates, found in foods such as pastas, dried beans, whole grains, cereals, corn, and rice. As discussed earlier, these foods are also rich in many essential vitamins and minerals.

On the other hand, says Carol Hodges, "contrary to popular belief, physical activity does not increase the need for protein, especially since most people in the country consume more than the recommended daily amount. Extra protein is converted to fat or energy and it doesn't make sense to load up on meat or protein supplements." One exception is athletes, such as body builders, wrestlers, and gymnasts, who are in the process of building increased muscle mass. They need more protein

The food stamp program has enabled many poor families to ensure that their children receive proper nutrition.

than most other people and protein supplements, in the form of powders or pills, can provide the extra protein without the fat and cholesterol found in protein-rich foods such as meat and dairy products. The low vitamin and mineral content of some protein supplements is not a matter of concern as long as the consumer takes in the proper amounts of these nutrients in his or her regular diet. Those who are unsure about

how to calculate the right balance of carbohydrates, proteins, and fats should consult a doctor.

Today, *where* people eat seems to have as much importance as *what* they eat. Changes in people's eating habits due to altered social and work patterns in the last 40 years have had a significant impact on health and nutrition in the United States and many other developed countries. The daily consumption of the right amounts of carbohydrates, proteins, and fats, and with them vitamins and minerals, was more certain in the days when the majority of people ate most of their meals at home. However, getting a healthy nutritional balance has become more difficult as increasing numbers of people have adopted life-styles emphasizing eating out. Carol Hodges comments that:

> there has been a marked increase in eating out or purchasing prepared foods to eat in. In either case, some people are eating more food prepared by others than by themselves. National Restaurant Association surveys [in the late 1980s] indicate that the average individual eats out about 3.7 times a week and that nearly 80 million customer transactions occur in commercial food service establishments each day. The association estimates that 40 percent of the food dollar is currently spent away from home. For some people—particularly businesspeople and others who travel frequently—as much as half their nutrition needs might be provided by the food service industry, primarily restaurants. . . . Researchers at Cornell University found that overall nutrient intake was lower for those persons eating meals away from home.

The increasing consumption of fast foods, especially by children and teenagers, whose growing bodies particularly need proper balances of vitamins, minerals, carbohydrates, proteins, and fats, also makes eating a healthy diet more difficult. Most fast foods do not contain enough fruits, vegetables, whole grains, and milk. According to Hodges:

> The typical meal of a burger, fried chicken, or fish, accompanied by french fries and a soft drink or shake is high in saturated fat, cholesterol, sodium, and refined carbohydrates [sugars with no nutritional value]. Pizza and other ethnic fast foods may have a slightly different nutrient composition, but most are still high in fat and sodium. . . . Overcooking, cooking and holding/reheating, soaking, and other preparation methods also detract from nutritional value.

Apparently then, millions of people rely heavily on eating prepared food outside the home without knowing the nutritional value, or lack thereof, of what they are consuming. In the face of so many uncertainties about food, the best way to ensure a balanced and healthy diet is to become educated about nutrition. The educated consumer who must eat out might substitute a lean piece of fish for a fatty hamburger, or an apple for a pile of greasy fries. And those who frequent restaurants might be more likely to ask their waiter or waitress about the ingredients in certain dishes, as well as how those dishes were prepared.

Harmful Habits and Nutrition

A number of other factors, including certain harmful and fairly common habits, affect the amounts of vitamins and minerals consumed and absorbed by the body. As mentioned earlier, smoking greatly hinders the absorption of vitamin C and also contaminates the body with lead and other toxic substances. Among these are nicotine, a powerfully addictive narcotic; carbon monoxide, a poisonous gas; and various tars and other chemicals. All of these substances counteract, to one degree or another, the healthful physical effects of vitamins and minerals. Smoking also accelerates the rate of oxidation in the body, working in direct opposition to vitamins E and C, which apparently work to slow this degenerative process.

The work of vitamins and minerals is also hindered by alcohol and other drugs. Excessive alcohol consumption reduces the body's supply of these nutrients because of the tendency of the drinker to substitute alcohol, which has no substantial nutritional value, for healthful foods. Thus, alcoholics are highly prone to developing vitamin deficiency diseases such as scurvy, night blindness, and pellagra. Caffeine, a drug found in coffee, tea, colas, and chocolate, can cause a loss of calcium from the body in some people and, therefore, sometimes speeds up the onset of osteoporosis. Marijuana, a widely used recreational drug, also works against the healthful effects of vitamins and minerals. Contrary to one popular belief, marijuana smoking is not a safe substitute for cigarette smoking, since marijuana smoke also contains many poison-

Drugs such as marijuana deplete the body of essential vitamins.

ous substances, impedes vitamin C absorption, and increases the rate of oxidation in the body.

Eating disorders involve other harmful practices that significantly affect the intake and absorption of vitamins, minerals, and other essential nutrients. The three major eating disorders presently recognized by doctors are *compulsive overeating,* bulimia, and anorexia. All of these are interrelated in the sense that they constitute varying reactions to the fear of becoming overweight. Many people with this fear attempt to lose weight by denying themselves food, that is, by going on severely restrictive reducing diets. Such diets have proven to be destructive rather than beneficial because sooner or later everyone gives in to the urge to eat. Unfortunately, a number of people respond to this urge by *binging,* or eating larger than normal amounts of food, food that is almost always high in fats, processed flours, and nutritionally valueless sugars. Single binges of 3,000 to 10,000 calories or more are not uncommon. These people, who usually binge at least twice a week or more for months, are called compulsive overeaters. Obviously, they pay little attention to the proper intake of vitamins and minerals and many suffer from mild but chronic cases of vitamin deficiency. Eventually, as their binging produces an inevitable weight gain, they stop binging and go on reducing diets again. After losing some or all of the weight, they then resume binging and the cycle repeats itself. Some compulsive overeaters eventually give up trying to diet, continue binging, and become *obese.*

Other compulsive overeaters carry their destructive eating pattern a step farther. They try to counteract the massive intake of food in their binges by vomiting, or *purging,* afterward, a disorder known as bulimia. Bulimics, who often also resort to laxatives and diuretics to get rid of food, may binge and purge from one or two times a week to several times a day. In addition to putting undo stress on the stomach and damaging the enamel of the teeth, the frequent vomiting eliminates large quantities of vitamins and minerals that would otherwise be absorbed by the body. As a result, chronic bulimics may suffer from the uncomfortable side effects of mild to moderate deficiencies of calcium, iron, vitamin C, and other nutrients.

Another eating disorder that develops among binge eaters is anorexia, characterized by self-starvation. For reasons that are still not entirely understood, most anorexics are women. Obsessed by their body image and extremely fearful of becoming overweight, anorexics try to overcome the effects of their occasional binging by going on prolonged and very restrictive reducing diets. Many anorexics may consume as little as 300 to 600 calories per day, or one-quarter or less the amount eaten by the average person. Almost all chronic anorexics drop below 100 pounds and many, as they use up all of their fat and begin to burn muscle tissue, reach weights of 70 pounds or less, requiring them to enter a hospital for treatment. It comes as no surprise that anorexics do not take in enough vitamins and minerals. Under their self-imposed condition of starvation, they may suffer from many of the same vitamin and deficiency conditions common in impoverished countries with high rates of malnutrition.

Education Is the Key

It is clear, then, that many potentially harmful factors influence the body's consumption of vitamins, minerals, and other important nutrients. Dealing with and overcoming these factors first requires recognizing and understanding them. Therefore, the key to acquiring and maintaining good health is education about nutrition. As Benjamin Burton points out:

> Adolescents are particularly in need of nutrition information. On the one hand, this age group is noted for its poor food habits; on the other, its nutritive requirements are greater than those of most adults. Girls are particularly affected since many of them compound the demands made by growth with the [physical] stress and strain of early pregnancies. At the same time most adolescents, having a strong interest in personal, physical improvement, represent a fertile field for the seeds of nutrition education.

Most experts agree that such nutritional education for young people should begin in the schools, especially in the primary grades. Parents

Children tend to eat on the run, making it especially difficult to provide them with well-balanced meals rich in vitamins and minerals.

should also contribute to young people's growing knowledge of nutrition, not only by providing nutritious meals at home, but also by periodically explaining about the importance and functions of vitamins, minerals, and other nutrients. Often, however, parents lack this information because their own educations in this area were lacking.

Therefore, it is vitally important for young people themselves to lead the way in improving the nutrition and health of society. This can be done through demonstrating concern for health and health issues, by reading books like this one and the others listed in the FURTHER READING section, and by using this concern and knowledge to build healthy eating habits. These habits, hopefully, will last a lifetime and set an example for future generations.

APPENDIX

FOR MORE INFORMATION

The following is a list of organizations and associations that can provide further information on the issues discussed in this book.

The American Dietetic Association
216 W. Jackson Blvd., Suite 800
Chicago, IL 60606-6995
(312) 899-0040

Anorexia Nervosa and Related Eating
    Disorders, Inc. (ANRED)
P.O. Box 5102
Eugene, OR 97405
(503) 344-1144

Center for Science in the Public
    Interest
1501 16th Street, NW
Washington, DC 20036

Food and Drug Administration
Office of Consumer Affairs
5600 Fishers Lane, HFE-88
Rockville, MD 20857
(301) 443-3170

Food and Nutrition Information Center
National Agricultural Library
10301 Baltimore Blvd., Room 304
Beltsville, MD 20705
(301) 344-3719

National Institute of Nutrition
1565 Carling Avenue, Suite 400
Ottawa, Ontario
KIZ 8RI
Canada
(613) 725-1889

Society for Nutrition Education
1700 Broadway
Oakland, GA 94612

U.S. Department of Agriculture
Human Nutrition Information Service
Nutrient Data Bank
Hyattsville, MD 20782

FURTHER READING

Bosco, Dominick. *The People's Guide to Vitamins and Minerals: From A to Zinc.* Chicago: Contemporary Books, 1980.

Boston Women's Health Book Collective. *The New Our Bodies, Ourselves.* New York: Simon & Schuster, 1992.

Brody, Jane. *Jane Brody's Nutrition Book.* New York: Bantam Books, 1977.

Burton, Benjamin T. *The Heinz Handbook of Nutrition.* New York: McGraw-Hill, 1965.

Carlson, Linda. *Food and Fitness.* Los Angeles: Price/Stern/Sloan, 1988.

Cowley, Geoffrey. "Vitamin E for a Healthy Heart." *Newsweek,* May 31, 1993.

———. "Vitamin Revolution." *Newsweek,* June 7, 1993.

Drews, Frederick R., et al. *A Healthy Life: Exercise, Behavior, Nutrition.* Indianapolis: Benchmark Press, 1986.

Dunn, Martha Davis. *Fundamentals of Nutrition.* Boston: CBI, 1983.

Epstein, Rachel. *Eating Habits and Disorders.* New York: Chelsea House, 1990.

Hodges, Carol A. *Culinary Nutrition for Foodservice Professionals.* New York: Van Nostrand Reinhold, 1989.

Krause, Marie V., and L. Kathleen Mahan. *Food, Nutrition and Diet Therapy.* Philadelphia: W. B. Saunders, 1979.

McDougall, John A., and Mary A. McDougall. *The McDougall Plan for Super Health and Life-Long Weight Loss.* Piscataway, NJ: New Century, 1983.

Nardo, Don. *Exercise.* New York: Chelsea House, 1992.

O'Neill, Cherry Boone. *Starving for Attention.* New York: Dell, 1982.

Rodale, J. I. *The Complete Book of Minerals for Health.* Emmaus, PA: Rodale Books, 1972.

Shils, Maurice E., and Vernon R. Young. *Modern Nutrition in Health and Disease.* Philadelphia: Lea & Febiger, 1988.

GLOSSARY

amino acids the chemical building blocks of proteins

anorexia (nervosa) an eating disorder characterized by poor self-image, self-starvation, and health-threatening weight loss

beriberi a disease caused by a deficiency of the vitamin thiamine

binging eating unusually large amounts of food in a single sitting

bulimia (nervosa) an eating disorder characterized by frequent binging and purging of foods

carotenes molecularly incomplete forms of vitamin A

catalyst a substance that retains its own physical characteristics while changing the speed and nature of a chemical reaction

cholesterol a white, fatty substance, found in meat and dairy products, that can coat and block the walls of the arteries and eventually cause a heart attack

compulsive overeating an eating disorder characterized by periods of frequent binging, followed by periods of dieting

DNA the chemical substance within cells that carries the genetic code

enzyme a substance that alters the structure of food molecules

epithelial tissues the topmost tissue layers both inside and outside the body

fat-soluble able to be dissolved in fat

goiter a condition, characterized by swelling of the thyroid gland, caused by a deficiency of the mineral iodine

gram a metric unit of mass equal to one-thousandth of a kilogram

hemoglobin an oxygen-bearing protein in red blood cells

hypercalcemia a condition caused by overconsumption of vitamin D and characterized by excess calcium in the blood

iodized combined with iodine

iron deficiency anemia a condition caused by a deficiency of iron in the blood

large macronutrients carbohydrates, proteins, and fats

macrominerals minerals needed by the body in quantities of 100 milligrams or more a day

megadose an extremely large dose

microgram one-millionth of a gram

microminerals minerals needed by the body in quantities of only a few grams or micrograms a day

milligram one-thousandth of a gram

myoglobin an oxygen-bearing substance in the muscle tissues

night blindness the inability of the eyes to adjust to dim illumination

nonorganic nonliving

obese weighing 20% or more above one's ideal weight

osteoporosis a condition caused by a deficiency of calcium, characterized by a reduction in the amount and strength of the bone tissues

oxidation a chemical process in which oxygen molecules combine with other substances

pellagra a disease caused by a deficiency of vitamin A

pigmentation coloring

polished rice rice that has had the nutrient-rich outer hulls removed

purging vomiting

rickets a disease caused by a deficiency of vitamin D

scurvy a disease caused by a deficiency of vitamin C

toxic poisonous

vitamins and minerals chemical compounds the body requires in small amounts to maintain regular health and promote growth and reproduction

water-soluble able to be dissolved in water

INDEX

Don Nardo is a filmmaker and composer, as well as an award-winning writer. He has written articles, short stories, and over 45 books, including *Lasers, Gravity, Animation, The War of 1812, Eating Disorders, Medical Diagnosis, Exercise,* and biographies of Charles Darwin, Thomas Jefferson, H. G. Wells, and Cleopatra. He has also written numerous screenplays and teleplays, including work for Warner Brothers and ABC television. Mr. Nardo lives with his wife, Christine, on Cape Cod, Massachusetts.

Dale C. Garell, M.D., is medical director of California Children Services, Department of Health Services, County of Los Angeles. He is also associate dean for curriculum at the University of Southern California School of Medicine and clinical professor in the Department of Pediatrics & Family Medicine at the University of Southern California School of Medicine. From 1963 to 1974, he was medical director of the Division of Adolescent Medicine at Children's Hospital in Los Angeles. Dr. Garell has served as president of the Society for Adolescent Medicine, chairman of the youth committee of the American Academy of Pediatrics, and as a forum member of the White House Conference on Children (1970) and White House Conference on Youth (1971). He has also been a member of the editorial board of the *American Journal of Diseases of Children.*

C. Everett Koop, M.D., Sc.D., is former Surgeon General, deputy assistant secretary for health, and director of the Office of International Health of the U.S. Public Health Service. A pediatric surgeon with an international reputation, he was previously surgeon-in-chief of Children's Hospital of Philadelphia and professor of pediatric surgery and pediatrics at the University of Pennsylvania. Dr. Koop is the author of more than 175 articles and books on the practice of medicine. He has served as surgery editor of the *Journal of Clinical Pediatrics* and editor-in-chief of the *Journal of Pediatric Surgery.* Dr. Koop has received nine honorary degrees and numerous other awards, including the Denis Brown Gold Medal of the British Association of Paediatric Surgeons, the William E. Ladd Gold Medal of the American Academy of Pediatrics, and the Copernicus Medal of the Surgical Society of Poland. He is a chevalier of the French Legion of Honor and a member of the Royal College of Surgeons, London.

PICTURE CREDITS